Saving

SAVANNAH

Saving
SAVANNAH

Tonya Bolden

BLOOMSBURY
NEW YORK   LONDON   OXFORD   NEW DELHI   SYDNEY

BLOOMSBURY YA
Bloomsbury Publishing Inc., part of Bloomsbury Publishing Plc
1385 Broadway, New York, NY 10018

BLOOMSBURY and the Diana logo are trademarks of Bloomsbury Publishing Plc

First published in the United States of America in January 2020 by Bloomsbury YA

Bloomsbury books may be purchased for business or promotional use.
For information on bulk purchases please contact Macmillan Corporate and
Premium Sales Department at specialmarkets@macmillan.com

Library of Congress Cataloging-in-Publication Data
Names: Bolden, Tonya, author.
Title: Saving Savannah / by Tonya Bolden.
Description: New York : Bloomsbury, 2020.
Summary: Savannah Riddle feels suffocated by her life as the daughter of an
upper-class African American family in Washington, DC, until she meets a
working-class girl named Nella, who introduces her to the suffragette and
socialist movements and to her politically active cousin Lloyd.
Identifiers: LCCN 2019019792 (print) | LCCN 2019022393 (e-book)
ISBN 978-1-68119-804-0 (hardcover) • ISBN 978-1-68119-805-7 (e-book)
Subjects: CYAC: Social classes—Fiction. | Suffragists—Fiction. | Socialism—Fiction. |
Race relations—Fiction. | African Americans—Fiction. | Washington (D.C.)—
History—20th century—Fiction.
Classification: LCC PZ7.B635855 Sav 2020 (print) | LCC PZ7.B635855 (e-book) |
DDC [Fic]—dc23
LC record available at https://lccn.loc.gov/2019019792
LC ebook record available at https://lccn.loc.gov/2019022393

Book design by Jeanette Levy
Typeset by Westchester Publishing Services
Printed and bound in the U.S.A. by Berryville Graphics Inc., Berryville, Virginia
2 4 6 8 10 9 7 5 3 1

All papers used by Bloomsbury Publishing Plc are natural, recyclable products
made from wood grown in well-managed forests. The manufacturing processes
conform to the environmental regulations of the country of origin.

To find out more about our authors and books visit
www.bloomsbury.com and sign up for our newsletters.

For my fiction editor, Mary Kate Castellani, who
believed in *Crossing Ebenezer Creek*

Saving

SAVANNAH

SHINE, DAUGHTER, SHINE!

When Mother surprised her with the outfit, Savannah was momentarily enchanted.

And utterly shocked.

Was this the same woman who not so long ago said, "Absolutely not!" to spat pumps with a high King Louis heel, to a touch of lip rouge? Who said, "Not in my lifetime!" to getting a Dutch bob?

Days later, Savannah wasn't one bit shocked that heads turned when she entered the banquet room, but she cringed at the memory of once enjoying such attention.

Behind Savannah and her parents were Yolande and hers. Savannah imagined Yolande beyond giddy, and Yolande's parents, Claire and Oscar Holloway, bursting with pride as they stepped deeper into the room.

It was a room hung with crimson-and-gold Chinese lanterns. Tall, thin crystal vases topped with white plumes streaming pearls served as sentinel, centerpiece at each of the sea of tables.

Snow-white damask tablecloths.

Gilt-rimmed porcelain plates.

Crimson napkins in standing fans.

Sterling silver Tiffany Florentine flatware and gilt rim glassware heightened the room's sparkle and shine.

"Savannah! How marvelous you look!" squealed Edna Fitzhugh.

Savannah was just poised to take her seat.

Julia LaMonte hurried over. "We've missed you *so* at the literary society!"

"And at my tea two weeks ago!" added Hyacinth Miller, bringing up the rear.

The gaggle of girls in silks and satins, organzas, taffetas, georgettes grew.

Inez Graham.

Rebecca Hawkins.

Alice Turner.

Ethel Bazemore.

Edna grabbed Savannah by the arm. "Let's get our photographs taken *now!*" She had Savannah fully in tow when—

"Wait a minute." Savannah wriggled free, turned back, beckoned to a woebegone Yolande staring at her water goblet. "Come on, Yolande," said Savannah. "Come."

The girls made a beeline for the corner of the room with panels of sheer white fabric illuminated from behind by strands of flame-shaped bulbs.

Savannah waved to the photographer, gave him her only genuine smile of the night. "Hi, Uncle Madison!"

"Hello there, Little Riddle! You look"—he kissed his thumb and forefinger—"*bellissimo!*"

Quick, quick he arranged the girls—shortest (Yolande) to tallest (Savannah)—into a pose.

"Lean slightly to your right, faces uplifted, world-class smiles!" He stepped behind his camera. "Hold, hold, hold!"

As Savannah *held*, *held*, *held*, she ached for enchantment all over again with her outfit. It really was splendid with its simple V-neck, a bead-flecked emerald-green velvet dress with an ankle-length balloon hemline. Her favorite part was the dreamy draped top layer of emerald-green chiffon bedecked with beaded oval medallions.

On her feet, silver satin dancing shoes.

On her arms, white evening gloves.

Tucked on one side of Savannah's sumptuous crown braid was a silver-and-rhinestone peacock-shaped hairpin, the bird's neck craning back. Another surprise from Mother. "The peacock is a symbol of renewal," she'd said.

Flash!

"One more," said Uncle Madison. "Hold, hold, hold!"

Flash!

"Now me and Savannah!" pleaded Edna.

"Hold, hold, hold!"

Flash!

"I get to have one with Savannah too!" said a pouting Inez. Then Hyacinth, Julia, Rebecca, Alice, Ethel. Yolande last.

"Hold, hold, hold!"

Flash!

Cary Sanderson, tall, lean, café au lait, swaggered over, waved Yolande aside. Nestled beside a dazed, still blinking Savannah, he slipped an arm around her waist. "Hello there, you."

"Hi, Cary." Her stomach was in knots.

"World-class smiles!"

Flash!

Cary whispered into Savannah's ear, gave her a squeeze, then strutted off to greet a friend.

∽⌒∾

"I can't believe we're really here!" chirped Yolande.

The girls snaked their way to their table in a now very crowded room, alive with so much chatter, chuckles, giggles, sounds of contentment.

"Remember how we used to jump up and down as our parents headed to this fete in their finest? 'One day us!' we shouted. Remember? We stepped so daintily around my parlor trying our best to look charming, elegant, practicing for the day when we—"

Savannah snickered. "I remember we had whoever was minding us make egg salad or cheese and cucumber tea sandwiches, then put on an apron and serve us in the dining room—and on the good china too. We threatened that if she didn't obey we'd say she'd throttled us."

Yolande stopped, rose on tiptoe, craned her neck. "Our

parents have already helped themselves. Let's go get some food."

Savannah looked right, left. Both endless buffets seemed laden with the same dishes.

Lobster tails, lobster salad, shrimp salad, shrimp cocktail, oysters and clams on the half shell, oysters Rockefeller, salmon mousse, poached salmon, deviled eggs, Duchess potatoes, Lobster Thermidor.

Savannah was sickened by the sight of so much food.

Prime rib, rack of lamb, leg of lamb, squab, ham timbales, Chiffonade salad, Waldorf salad, asparagus tips, crab cakes, crab puffs, radish roses, cucumber roses, celery boats stuffed with cream cheese, manzanillos stuffed with nuts, with peppers.

"You don't look hungry." Yolande was practically licking her lips.

Petit fours, macaroons, melon balls, chocolate-covered strawberries, jelly creams, meringues.

Savannah settled on a single-rib lamb chop and a Duchess potato. Yolande's plate was a crowd of crab puffs.

"Having a good time, girls?" asked Yolande's father, ginger-haired, could pass if he wished.

"Best time ever!" said Yolande.

"And you?" asked Yolande's mother, a gazelle-like chocolate beauty.

Savannah flashed the requisite smile. "Best time ever."

"Shine, daughter, shine!" Father had belted out as they left the house that evening. He, hair salt and pepper well beyond his temples, in tuxedo with tails, silver vest, high-stand wing-tip collared shirt, top hat. Doe-eyed Mother, sandy hair with streaks of gray swept up in a mature woman's Gibson, did look stunning, Savannah had to admit. Her silver lamé-and-mesh gown was gorgeous. So too Mother's slate evening coat with its pattern of peacock feathers in a delicate dance. And Mother did sound more earnest than pushy when she said, "This night will do you so much good!"

For weeks Savannah had struggled to churn up the courage to tell her parents that she did *not* want to go to the Sanderson fete. Time and again, she vowed to make her stand over break-fast, over dinner, but . . .

Then two days before the gala, as she and Mother sat in the Madeline Beauty Parlor waiting their turns for facial massages, manicures, washes and sets—

"Mother," Savannah began, eyes cast on the checkerboard floor.

"Yes, my darling girl?"

Once again Savannah chickened out.

The thought of disappointing Yolande—a twinge of guilt.

The thought of disappointing Mother not a whit.

But wiping a smile off Father's face . . .

"Shine, daughter, shine!" he always said before a ballet recital, her face cupped in his hands, a kiss planted on her forehead.

Out on stage with his praise and love hugging her heart, Savannah was a bright and shining star with every plié, piqué, and pirouette, with every grand jeté.

She knew how much Father looked forward to arriving at the Sanderson fete with Mother on one arm, her on the other.

So she went.

So she did her utmost to shine.

When Uncle Madison said "Hold, hold, hold!"

When overwhelmed by that obscene buffet.

When she surveyed people puffed up, preening, jockeying to pose beside Mrs. La-Di-Da, Mr. So-and-So.

Flash!

Savannah managed to shine when that fella with a wicked smile, with eyes that hypnotize led his band onto the stage.

When The Duke's Serenaders, dressed to the nines, launched into a toe-tapping rendition of "Hindustan," Savannah found herself softly singing. Maybe she'd find renewal in the night after all.

Camel trappings jingle,
Harp-strings sweetly tingle,
With a sweet voice mingle,
Underneath the stars . . .

In back-to-back dance requests Savannah sought to lose

herself in the Castle Walk's dips and rises, glides, hesitation steps, in the Two-Step's slow, then quick moves, spins, and swings.

Though breathless and queasy, when Cary Sanderson took her by the hand Savannah let him take her into a tango.

A figure eight.

But then, a beat before the close—

The chatter, chuckles, giggles, those sounds of content- ment became a deafening crescendo. All that sparkle and shine as blinding as a high-noon summer sun.

And Cary—with his parents' wealth, good looks, expen- sive suits, prospects for Amherst, mapped-out life—no heft, no depth to him.

"I'm sorry, Cary, I can't—"

Savannah slipped the sterling silver friendship ring from her finger, pressed it into Cary's hand.

Stares.

Glares.

Mouths agape.

Savannah didn't, couldn't care. She fled from the dance floor to her table.

"I need some air."

"Shall I come with you?" That was Mother with furrowed brow.

"No, no, I'm fine. I simply need some air."

Yolande rose.

Savannah grabbed her evening purse—beads, sequins, a peacock eye appliqué. "Some air and some time alone."

Savannah raced to the cloakroom for her silver brocade cape, then flashed down the corridor.

"Thank you," she said to the doorman, whisking through the outer doors.

There was frost in the air.

Staring up at the stars, Savannah ached for the strength, the freedom to scream. She paced instead.

The minutes a weight. Time a tease.

She checked her sterling silver bracelet watch. At least another hour.

Back inside, Savannah walked stiffly past the billiard room, lounge, gift shop, meeting room, smaller banquet room, past a boy in a bellhop's uniform perched upon a stool.

She stopped at the plush pink roundabout, eased down.

Waiters fleet of feet passed in and out of swinging doors, hurried upstairs, down.

An arrogant-looking man walked the corridor until he didn't.

"Are you all right, miss?"

"Yes, I'm fine, thank you."

"You are a guest of the Sandersons, yes?"

"Yes."

"Can we get you anything?"

She *was* thirsty. "Perhaps a ginger ale."

Mr. Arrogant snapped his fingers at that boy perched upon a stool.

The kid jumped down, stood at attention, and Savannah saw him tremble. He looked petrified, as if one wrong move—

Savannah cleared her throat. "Sir, never mind about that ginger ale, but thank you." Minutes later she rose, returned to a night with frost in the air.

CRAB PUFF AFTER CRAB PUFF

Only one girl complimented her on her royal-blue taffeta dress: the one they called Beanstalk Belinda behind her back.

Wall-eyed Winston Smith and Theophilus Graham with horrible breath were the only boys who asked her to dance.

She spent so much, too much of the evening fielding questions that had nothing to do with *her*.

"Where is Savannah?"

"Has Savannah fallen ill?"

"What on earth happened to Savannah?"

When not responding with a shrug, Yolande ate crab puff after crab puff.

THE WATCH FIRE WOMEN

That was *so* embarrassing!"

Savannah glanced out her window, envied rays straining through mottled sky.

The Riddles and the Holloways had walked home in silence that Friday night. And Savannah knew that Yolande would show up the next day to squawk.

Thin feet welded to the floor, spindly arms at her sides, fists clenched, Yolande stood fuming, pale cheeks flaming red. "It was just plain *rude*! You simply can't do things like—"

Can't.

Mustn't.

Oughtn't

Shouldn't.

Savannah was so sick of such words—leashes, chains, vises.

"*The* event of the year! Only the best of us were invited."

"Perhaps that's the problem." Savannah fingered the pencil tucked into the thick plait that fell a long ways down her back. She eyed the sketch pad she'd tossed on her desk when Yolande marched into her room.

"What are you talking about? What problem?"

"Nothing."

Savannah slumped into her desk chair that faced the window.

Yolande stamped her foot. "I try, Savannah. I really do, but I just don't understand you."

Makes two of us.

The French window whistled with the wind.

"The title of this year's fete was *Excelsior!*"

Pause.

"It means onward and upward!"

"I know what *Excelsior* means."

"You don't act like it."

Yolande began to pace. "Onward and upward, Savannah! The Great War is over! Onward and upward, for heaven's sake!"

Savannah was snatched back to news she had gorged on in the *Bee*, the *Post*, the *Herald*, the *Star*. Never before had she paid such close attention to the news. Never before been so swallowed up.

"U.S. AT WAR WITH GERMANY; PRESIDENT SIGNS RESOLUTION."

"Children the Pitiful Victims of Modern War's Ruthlessness."

"INSANITY INCREASE ATTRIBUTED TO WAR."

"13 MILLION MEN IS COST OF WAR."

Savannah also went back to the passage of the Espionage Act, the Sedition Act, back to Yolande's feeble attempt at comfort. "Father says we'll be fine so long as we don't say any-thing bad about the government or anything else American, so long as we don't associate with people who do."

And those accursed 4-Minute Men! Just when Savannah was about to lose herself in a photoplay, on came the lights and a 4-Minute Man stepped onto the stage.

"Ladies and gentlemen, I ask for just four minutes of your time . . ."

To warn of German spies.

To preach the gospel of Liberty Bonds.

"Onward and upward," Yolande whined. "Do you hear me, Savannah? Not only is the Great War over, but reports of Spanish flu are doing nothing but going down."

More headlines flashed across Savannah's mental sky.

"SCANDINAVIA IS SWEPT BY 'SPANISH INFLUENZA.'"

"SPANISH INFLUENZA SPREADING IN D.C."

The city had been a ghost town. Schools and libraries closed. Public gatherings banned.

Even after things opened back up, nothing was normal; still they lived in the shadow of death.

Streets graveyard quiet.

White gauze masks.

Flannel bags of camphor dangling around necks.

Yolande was pacing again. "The Sanderson party was a great big wonderful way to celebrate that so much *awfulness* is over! No more Meatless Mondays. No more Wheatless Wednesdays! No more victory gardens! No more stupid signs fussing about not wasting food."

Food.

Frankfurter out. Hot dog in. Or better yet, Liberty sausage.

Hamburger out. Liberty steak in.

Sauerkraut out. Liberty cabbage in.

Oh, no, wait, said the *Bee*, for one, giving sauerkraut a reprieve: "As a matter of fact, the dish is said to be of Dutch, rather than of German origin."

"Think *Excelsior!*," Yolande pleaded. "Think onward and upward!"

Onward Savannah had gone to the Y solo so many Saturdays to pack comfort kits with soap, toothbrushes, toothpaste, shaving cream, razors, Prince Albert tobacco, pipe cleaners, Juicy Fruit, figs, chocolate. To roll bandages, knit socks . . . for men overseas up against strafing, machine gun fire, flamethrowers, suffering trench foot, shattered legs, blown-off jaws. How much comfort did a kit bring? Could it keep a man from going mad?

"Why do you insist on being so glum?" Yolande plopped down on the chaise.

"You've not kept up with the news?"

"What news?"

"More anarchist bombs!"

"That wasn't *here*, that was in Philadelphia. And *weeks* ago."

"And what about what has happened *here*—in front of the White House?"

"White women have been picketing there for, what, two years now? Everybody knows that."

Savannah snatched up from her desk a weeks-old *Star*, waved it in Yolande's face. "On New Year's day they lit an urn—a watch fire for freedom—vowed to keep it burning until the Anthony amendment gets through. But then—"

"Yes, I know, I know, there was a bit of a ruckus."

"A *bit* of a ruckus?" Savannah shook her head. "Boys, even *grown* men, threw stones at the women! Some were dragged across the pavement and hauled off to jail!"

"Hasn't that happened before?"

"Yes, but that it should *keep* happening is . . ."

Yolande was hopeless.

Unfazed.

Unmoved.

Except by the likes of crab puffs.

So shallow.

And she just wouldn't shut up! "So maybe it's a good thing those Alice Paul people want little to do with Negro women. Mother said years ago they expected Ida Wells-Barnett to travel all the way here from Chicago to march in the *back* of their parade."

"I know that."

The window whistled again, and Savannah was two seconds from telling Yolande to buzz off.

Yolande shot up. "You *abandoned* me last night!" Again she stamped her feet. "After you left, it was awful. I was so—so—"

Savannah drummed her fingers on her sketch pad. "You really need to have more faith in yourself, Yolande. I can't forever be your *crutch*." She snatched her white Shetland shawl from the back of her desk chair, wrapped it over her sky-blue jumper dress, grabbed her sketch pad. Within a few steps she was through the French doors and out onto her small balcony, knowing Yolande wouldn't follow, given her trouble with heights.

With a flip, the sketch pad open.

With a pluck from her plait, the pencil in hand.

Savannah picked up where she left off with her skyline. Across the top—

Saturday, February 1, 1919.

She stepped closer to the wrought iron curlicue railing, stared down.

Father's black Buick.

Old man Boudinot's Saxon Roadster.

Mrs. Pinchback, coat collar up, was walking her Yorkshire terrier, Sebastian. He yapped, yapped, yapped at the wind. It had been months since Savannah had seen a smile on Mrs. Pinchback's face. Still mourning her nephew.

Looking up, out, Savannah returned to her sketch, to townhouse turrets and gables, treetops, Millet post streetlamps.

She faced the 900 block of M Street NW again, her skyline again.

If only Yolande would leave. Savannah hoped silence would do the trick.

"I guess I'll be going," Yolande finally said.

Seconds later, Savannah flipped to a fresh page of her sketch pad. Across the top she wrote *The Watch Fire Women*.

BEGGAR IN THE RAIN

It was like water slipping through her fingers steadily, daily, and Yolande couldn't fathom life without the friendship.

Their homes side by side.

Birthdays a week apart.

Their monthlies came a day apart.

And they were both miracle babies.

Yolande remembered them scampering up to her mother's sewing room, finding the key to the rosewood sewing box, picking the ideal needle, pricking each other's thumbs.

"Sisters!"

Blood touching blood.

"I want my friend *back*!" Yolande muttered outside the Riddle townhouse all those years later on that February 1919 day.

Back.

Where was the Savannah who loved sledding like lightning down snowy I-Dare-You Hill with her mother nowhere in sight and Yolande keeping her secret?

Where was the Savannah who laughed so hard at Charlie Chaplin photoplays that she got stitches in her sides, who savored marshmallow roasts and ghost stories as darkness crept up on clambakes?

At least they still walked to, from school together.

But no longer arm in arm.

At least they still kept company some weekday afternoons.

But Saturdays together were rare.

Entering her home, Yolande was flooded by memories of the once-upon-a-time sweet, smooth rhythm and rhyme of their lives.

Skipping rope.

Hopscotch.

Strolling down the street with the Brownie cameras Charlie sent one Christmas, taking photographs of each other, of maples, lindens, that box of kittens inside old man Boudinot's gate, the Pinchbacks' Sebastian straining at the leash, yapping at a stranger.

Too cold, too hot, rainy, or with dusk begun . . .

Chinese checkers.

Spillikins.

Crafting cat's cradles.

Fashioning stories about the families dwelling in their twin dollhouses.

Sisters.

They had vowed that when they grew up, they'd marry fellas from the finest of families, fellas who were best friends, and they'd make them buy homes side by side. Savannah would name her first baby girl Yolande. Yolande would name hers Savannah.

"We'll give them both the middle name Marie!" Savannah had said.

"Fat chance now," Yolande whispered with a sigh. There was no friendship ring on her horizon, and Savannah, who could take her pick of real catches, well, she had gone and ended it with Cary Sanderson.

Yolande entered her home pining for the past.

For photoplays at the Hiawatha.

Sundaes or ice cream sodas at Board's Drug Store.

Lunch at Lee's Lunch Room or better yet at Gaskins'— all by themselves.

Like clockwork it used to be. At noon through their front doors they stepped in matching outfits, maybe middy sailor dresses or shepherd's check suiting.

Now, time and again—for months—Yolande felt like a beggar in the rain when Mrs. Riddle answered the door, informed her that Savannah had already gone out.

If Savannah *was* home and if she *did* invite her in, after limp pleasantries Yolande was left to fiddle with time by reading a book, a *Saturday Evening Post*, dreaming up stories around the thistles and blooms on Savannah's yellow wallpaper.

Or watching Savannah sketch.

"I'm back, Mother!"

"In the kitchen, dear. Would you like some cocoa?"

"Yes, please."

You really need to have more faith in yourself, Yolande.

"Easy for you to say," Yolande mumbled, entering the kitchen. She didn't have willowy Savannah's beacon-light smile, didn't have her big beautiful eyes, nor that wondrous coppery skin, didn't walk with a royal's grace.

"I don't understand it, Mother," whimpered Yolande, staring at her cocoa's waning wisps of steam. "Savannah has become impossible!"

STARLIGHT

The women small, the banners large.

MR. PRESIDENT, HOW LONG MUST WOMEN WAIT FOR LIBERTY?

MR. PRESIDENT, WHAT WILL YOU DO FOR WOMAN SUFFRAGE?

Thinking about that insult to Ida Wells-Barnett, Savannah erased the words on one banner and replaced them with ALICE PAUL, WHEN WILL YOU PICKET AND PARADE AGAINST THE COLOR LINE?

And when will I really snap out of it!

Savannah quit her balcony, went to her desk.

From the bottom drawer she grabbed a bunch of newspaper clippings. In no time at all, every article, every bit of grim, grisly news lay in shreds in the wastepaper basket next to her desk.

The Great War, Spanish flu, East Saint Louis—gone!

Next, to her chiffonier where months ago—over a year ago—she had tucked in its mirror's frame a somber photograph from Charlie.

Row after row after row . . .

Negro men in Sunday best black suits, black hats.

Negro women and children in white.

One banner pleaded "MAKE AMERICA SAFE FOR DEMOCRACY."

Another scolded "RACE PREJUDICE IS THE OFF-SPRING OF IGNORANCE AND THE MOTHER OF LYNCHING."

"Except for muffled drumbeats, it was bone quiet," Charlie had written of the NAACP's Silent Parade triggered by East Saint Louis atrocities.

In response to her bitter tears over the reports of those beatings, stabbings, bludgeonings, of homes set ablaze, homes shot up as families slept, children hurled into flames—there was Yolande trying to change the subject, trying to comfort her with yet another bromide. "Mother says thank heavens we live in the capital, where, yes, we have to contend with the color line, but the whitefolks here are not nearly so barbaric."

Savannah took down the Silent Parade photograph, placed it in a desk drawer. In a quick glance out her window, she saw straining rays had conquered clouds.

Out of that Shetland shawl and sky-blue jumper dress.

Into her cinnamon walking suit, black boots, and black sealskin short-brimmed hat.

"I'm going out for a bit." She was standing in the doorway of the living room.

Mother sat on the davenport reading a book. Father in the arm rocker with the *Bee*.

"Where to?" asked Mother, looking up from her book.

"Just for a walk."

Mother pursed her lips. "Is Yolande going with you?"

"No."

"Did you invite her?"

"No."

Father rested the *Bee* on his lap, glanced at the brass-cased clock on the fireplace mantel.

"I won't be out long."

"But where's your coat?" asked Mother.

Savannah tugged on the front pockets of her suit jacket. "This *is* wool. And it's not that cold out."

"I'm well aware that it is wool, but I also know that the weather is fickle these days. The temperature could drop by the time you are returning home. You *mustn't* go out without a coat."

"But, Mother—"

Father looked at Savannah over his glasses.

Minutes later Savannah left the house with her black serge overcoat buttoned up to her neck.

She shed it once off her block, slung it over an arm.

"Hello, Savannah!"

"Hello, Mrs. Lane."

"Hi, Savannah!"

"Well, hello there, Jimmy Wiggins."

A dour man tipped his homburg. "Good day to you, Miss Riddle."

"Good day, Dr. Woodson."

She had never seen a smile on that man's face. If she kept on as she was, would she wind up a sour-face too?

I don't want that!

If only she could find delight in the likes of crab puffs.

Savannah felt more pep in her step nearer to U Street, that hub of pride with its movie theaters and restaurants, old man Boudinot's bookshop, the Underdown delicatessen, the Murray Brothers Printing company, Ware's, the Madeline Beauty Parlor, Uncle Madison's shop.

And being around Uncle Madison was like being around Charlie.

A little.

Where's Charlie?

Years back, she had scurried upstairs, downstairs, searched every room.

Where's Charlie?

Even checked closets.

Where's Charlie?

Heartsick and whimpering.

Charlie had been writing more often and, as always, sent a photograph. They scheduled telephone time for when Mother and Father would be out.

One time—

"Oh, Charlie, Cary is *insufferable*. The other day at the Fitzhughs' lawn party I overheard him boasting about his mother surprising him with *three* new dress suits."

Another—

"I don't know what's wrong with me—all I know is I'm not happy!"

Savannah had puzzled over why Charlie had begun to pay her more attention, then chalked it up to worry about Spanish flu.

Charlie . . .

It seemed ages since Father packed her and Mother up in the black Buick and drove to New York City where he had business. The nearer to the city, the thicker the tension in the car, the heavier the silence.

From the back seat Savannah imagined a sneer on Mother's face as they pulled up to a storefront on West 135th Street. On either side of the door a display case with urns, fans, other props. Stenciled in white in each window: CHARLESTON RIDDLE PHOTO STUDIO.

Two boys raced by on roller skates.

Mother shook her head, then once inside looked around as if a health inspector.

Charlie came out from the back room, looking like Father

spit him out as always. Both tall. Angular. Charlie had Father's dark, velvety skin, too, along with that look of purpose in his eyes. And he sported a razor-thin mustache just like Father. His hair was pomaded. He had on a nice suit. How Savannah wished she looked more like Father and Charlie, less like Mother.

Charlie and Father shook hands, embraced.

Charlie kissed Mother, left cheek, right cheek, then scooped up Savannah in his arms, "And ten hugs for you, Sis!"

"Certainly much larger than your first studio," said Father.

"It is that."

"And where do you live?" asked Mother with a sniff.

"Upstairs."

Things were tense still during dinner at the Empire— "the largest and finest Negro restaurant in Harlem," Charlie had said.

Father talked about expanding into the Northeast, starting with an office in New York, at which point Mother glared at Charlie, then changed the subject to saving Frederick Douglass's estate. "It will take years to bring his Cedar Hill back into its original glory, but we will do it!" Mother's face had softened.

Whenever Charlie got a word in edgewise, he spoke about the lectures he attended. He also talked about events he covered for the *New York Age* as if he didn't know that would get on Mother's nerves. Or maybe he didn't care, thought Savannah.

"Hello there, Savannah!"

"Hello there, Mrs. Crane."

Walking on, Savannah fumed all over again about Mother's badgering years back.

You know you are breaking your father's heart.

But, Mother . . .

You should not be throwing your life away.

But, Mother . . .

I am not asking you to give it up. It makes a perfectly fine hobby.

But, Mother . . .

Your father's firm offers safety and security.

But, Mother . . .

When Savannah reached 900 U Street NW, she looked up at the sign—SPURLOCK PHOTO STUDIO—that would have read SPURLOCK & RIDDLE PHOTO STUDIO had Mother not driven Charlie away.

In the display case, Uncle Madison's usual mix of prominent race men and women, alive and dead—Booker T. Washington, Dr. W. E. B. Du Bois, Mary Church Terrell—with photos of everyday people, like Annie Brooks Evans, like little girls lined up at a ballet bar and little boys in Sunday best posed against a car.

And the door was locked.

Hands formed into blinders, Savannah pressed her face to the glass.

She checked her bracelet watch.

Late lunch?

She rang the bell.

Face to the glass again, then to the street. "Shucks!"

Just as she was about to head off, the door opened.

"Well, well, if it isn't the Little Riddle! Twice in two days!"

He was the only person who could make a joke of her name and get away with it. Unlike Lafayette Mercer with his stupid taunts of "Riddle, can you fiddle?" For that he got a punch.

Once inside Uncle Madison's shop, Savannah frowned.

His shirtsleeves were unevenly rolled up, his tie unloosed. His gray trousers had smudges of plaster, flecks of paint. He had cobwebs in his hair.

"Are you all right?"

Uncle Madison looked himself over. "I was just sorting some things in the storeroom. Excuse me a minute while I tidy myself." Once he was through the door at the rear of the shop, Savannah sauntered over to the setup not far from that door. Savannah wondered if the tableau was for his last shoot or for one upcoming.

Against a black velvet backdrop were silver and gold crescents and full moons in a sea of tiny rhinestone stars. More black velvet on the floor and on it a domed, silver satin chair, a porter's chair transformed into a throne.

"And what do you call this one?"

A tidied Uncle Madison was back in the main room. He did a tap step, made ta-da hands. "Starlight."

"Nice." Savannah strolled around the room.

"So what brings you here?"

"Just felt like a walk."

Overcoat hung on the coatrack by the door, Savannah pulled out an envelope from her purse, waved Uncle Madison over to a small settee and table near the window. "And to show you two of Charlie's from a while back."

First photo: "That's the Nail and Parker Building. Both Negroes, and Charlie says they own a lot of real estate in Harlem."

"Wow!" said Uncle Madison. "Almost an entire block, six stories. Impressive!"

"And Harlem, he says, is fast becoming the mecca."

"So I've heard, so I've—Is this . . . ?"

Savannah had just handed him the second photograph. "Villa Lewaro. Charlie was hired for Madam Walker's Christmas party."

"Sublime!"

"Marble *everywhere*, Charlie said. Sculptures . . . I think thirty-four rooms. Her huge library has books bound in Moroccan leather." Savannah caught herself sounding like Yolande. Shallow. "That was the only room Charlie really cared for. All in all he found Madam Walker's mansion rather gaudy."

"To each his own," replied Uncle Madison.

"Charlie says he might visit this spring. But I'm not getting my hopes up. Last year he said he'd come for Christmas."

"And I'm sorry, Little Riddle, that it's been so long since we've had one of our secret lunches."

Savannah shrugged. "That's okay."

Those lunches had started not long after Charlie began writing and telephoning more.

Uncle Madison laid the photographs on the table. "You want to talk about last night?"

"No."

"I think you do."

Savannah let out a sigh for the ages. "I'm just so *tired* of, *embarrassed* by society. Such excess, such extravagance . . . But I saw you kept plenty busy."

"The Sandersons always have a long list of shots they want. Guests want photographs of themselves, ones with other guests, ones with their hosts, of course. And they all want multiple copies of each so they can—"

"Show off."

"More to it than that, I think."

Savannah rolled her eyes. "What more could there be?"

"To inspire. So people perhaps not so well off can see what's possible."

"That it's possible to have nice cars, fancy clothes, go to lavish parties? Shouldn't life be about more than that?"

"Would you rather you lived in a shack with an outhouse out back?"

"DO NOT tell me how much I have to be grateful for!"

"But you do."

"I know it," said Savannah through gritted teeth. "I know it, I know it, I know it! I'm not ungrateful. I'm simply . . ."

"The Sandersons, your parents, everybody else there last

night—these people have worked darn hard for what they have. Why shouldn't they cherish photographs trumpeting their success?"

Savannah looked at the back of Uncle Madison's head, plucked out a remaining cobweb.

"In the white press, how are we usually seen?"

"Sambo. Mammy. Criminals."

"And dumb as a brick. Most whitefolks don't want people like the Sandersons or the Riddles for that matter to exist. Let the world believe we're *all* servants, sharecroppers, and such." He took Savannah's hands in his. "Promise me you won't think too harshly of people who want photographs of themselves at a fabulous fete." Uncle Madison cupped a hand to an ear. "I can't hear you."

Savannah smiled. "Promise."

"Besides, you seem mighty proud of Charlie's photographs. Why's that?"

"That's different. That's art."

"And the photographs I took at the Sandersons' are . . . ?"

Savannah looked away.

"Understand that they are dreaming a world, encouraging others to dream too."

"At school no one dreams of anything of substance. Dances, fashion, gossip. Girls scheming on who they want to marry. Boys obsessed with taking over their fathers' businesses or making a killing in something else."

"To each his own, Savannah." Madison frowned. "Besides,

I find it hard to believe that *everyone* at Dunbar is like that. You're speaking of the circle you swim in, am I right?"

"Maybe."

"And maybe you need to widen your world."

"I just don't want to go to Howard!" Savannah blurted out. "And I don't want to marry the likes of Cary Sanderson!"

"*Whoa!* Where did that come from?"

Savannah shot up, stalked away, plopped down in the chair behind Uncle Madison's very messy desk. "How do you find anything?"

"Believe it or not, Little Riddle, I have a system!"

Savannah burst out laughing. "System, yeah right!"

Uncle Madison joined her at the desk. "Do you remember *anything* I said to you the last time we had lunch?"

"I know, I know. 'There has never been a time when there wasn't misery in the world *somewhere.*'"

He waved his hands in the air. "If I didn't have this, I don't think I'd be able to get out of bed in the morning!" After a pause he added, "As I told you, Little Riddle, you need a passion, a challenge."

"I won first prize in an essay contest at school. I wrote about man's inhumanity to man."

"Good for you!" He patted her on the back. "But does that really qualify as a challenge? Isn't it just doing more of what you're good at?"

"Now wait a minute!"

"Not a putdown. It's just that everything has always come *easy* for you, Savannah."

"I had a terrible time learning to ride a bike. It took *forever*, and you and Charlie were both so patient."

Uncle Madison frowned. "You learned in a matter of a day—hours, I think."

Savannah puzzled. She was certain that it had been a struggle.

"Did your mother ever find out, by the way?"

Savannah shook her head.

"Anyway," said Uncle Madison, "back to you. Have you ever failed a course?"

"No."

"And friends? Did you ever have to make friends?"

"Why, of course—"

"No, no. I didn't ask if you *have* friends. Have you ever had to make an effort to get people to like you, to want to be around you? Hasn't it always been moths to a flame?"

Savannah lowered her head.

"Look at me."

Reluctantly Savannah obliged, looked up into Uncle Madison's probing eyes.

He arched an eyebrow, tapped his Charlie Chaplin mustache. "A challenge, Little Riddle, a challenge, a passion, that's what you need. I say your problem is that you're bored. Purpose is a powerful antidote to the doldrums. Get engaged with something, take hold of life, stop being a mere observer."

He riffled through papers, found his appointment book, flipped through it. "So what is it that you want to do after high school?"

Savannah shrugged again, made a cat's cradle of her hands. "I don't know—well, yes, I do. I want to move to Harlem, be with Charlie."

"Are you really that angry with your parents?"

"I'm not angry with—well, I'm not angry with Father."

Uncle Madison glanced at his wristwatch. "My next appointment will be here soon, so—"

"I'll be getting along."

"Not necessary." He walked to the front of the shop, rolled down his shirt sleeves, buttoned his cuffs, grabbed his jacket from the coatrack. "It's light enough yet. Stay at the desk. Look like you're doing bookkeeping or something so the customer won't feel, you know, self-conscious or something."

Given the set, those moons and stars, that silver throne, Savannah expected someone in showbiz. A member of a jazz band, like one of The Duke's Serenaders. Maybe even Duke Ellington himself.

If not a musician maybe a singer or dancer. Perhaps a vaudeville act. Or the type of man who wears bespoke suits and a chinchilla coat, sports a diamond pinkie ring. When he laughs or smiles wide you see a gold tooth. He struts about U Street with a flashy lady on each arm.

She never imagined a silver-haired, elderly woman.

Her black dress, black walking coat were simple but expensive, Savannah knew. The wearer, a sprite of a woman, was frail but erect. When she lifted her veil—what fiery, what ancient eyes. If sketching her, Savannah would render her queen of a magical realm. The silver throne, the moons, the stars, they suited her to a tee.

Uncle Madison led the woman behind a curtain. "Just a dab of rouge," Savannah heard him say. "Just a touch of powder." He soon escorted her to the throne, then repositioned lights, adjusted the tripod, fiddled with the camera.

Savannah spied the woman staring at her.

Shoot done and the woman's makeup removed, Uncle Madison helped his customer over to a small writing table and wicker chair. "The other day," he asked, "when you made the appointment did you say you had only recently moved to the capital?"

"Only passing through, son. Here until Tuesday next."

"And you're staying at . . . ?"

"Mrs. Bennett's Boarding House on T Street."

"Savannah, hand me an invoice pad."

As she did, Savannah saw the woman staring at her again. Harder.

"You want five cabinet cards and twenty-five postcards, yes?" asked Uncle Madison.

"Yes, my dear."

Savannah watched Uncle Madison do the tallies in

his head, then fill out the top of the form. "Delivery to Mrs. Bennett's?"

"Yes, my dear."

Savannah took sneak peeks at the woman as she wrote out a check, rose, stepped over to her. "If you don't mind my asking, my dear, what is your full name?"

"Savannah Riddle, ma'am."

The woman clutched the pearl-and-diamond butterfly brooch pinned to her high-neck collar. Eyes went tender, misted up. "What a lovely encounter this has been," she whispered. "A lovely encounter indeed."

"My, my." Uncle Madison seemed truly pleased as he scanned his desk. "Good work!"

Checks matched with invoices stamped PAID.

Invoices not paid organized into subsets: 90 days, 60 days, 30 days due.

Price lists in one neat stack.

Savannah was proud of her work. Like times, long ago, on a day of no school, when she went with Father to his office. Seated on his swivel chair she tidied his gigantic desk with its sorters, books, pads, and mounds of paper in a room crowded with filing cabinets, bookcases, storage cabinets, a letter-copying press upon a safe, and people at desks, men scribbling, others on the telephone or talking into a dictating machine, women making Underwood typewriters clack, clack, clack.

"You should come around more often." Uncle Madison rubbed his chin. "Part-time job, maybe? You could even start to learn the trade. Of course your mother would have me flogged."

Savannah smiled, tilted her head to one side. "I don't think so—I mean, if you ever need me to help out . . . but I don't want to learn photography. I don't want to follow in Charlie's footsteps. I need to find my own."

SO MEAN TO ME

Dear Uncle Charlie,

I am once again writing to let you know that Savannah isn't any better. She is still so down in the mouth most times. Yesterday she gave Cary back his friendship ring and ran out of the Sanderson gala. Can you believe that? And earlier today she was so mean to me.

I am hoping that maybe you can . . .

Months back, when Savannah was out on her balcony sketching, Yolande had spied a letter from Charlie, scribbled his address into her notebook.

HELL FIGHTERS

Two Saturdays later, Savannah stared blankly out the kitchen window at the dusting of snow, mindlessly washing blue willow breakfast dishes, searching her mind for something new to do.

A challenge.

A passion.

A knock on the back door.

On the other side grinned a grimy boy in run-down shoes, a man's waistcoat over a pilly jacket, and moth-eaten pants. His cap, pushed back, was tattered.

"Miss Gertie Walcott send me. She say to give wunna dis." The boy reached into his pocket, brought out a small envelope. It was grimy, too, but the penmanship of the *Mrs. Riddle* was perfect.

The boy removed his cap, grinned wider.

"And what's your name?"

The boy thumped his chest. "I name Bim."

"Well, you stay right there, Bim."

At the cabinet where Mother kept a Lord Calvert tin of coins, Savannah thought to fish out a nickel, then changed her mind. Back at the door she handed Bim a dime.

"Tank you, Miss Fine Lady!" The boy beamed as if handed two fistfuls of gold.

"Oh, dear," said Mother. "Mrs. Walcott is ill. Her daughter, Nella, will come in her stead. Only she can't come until this evening."

When Savannah entered the room, Mother was flicking through her wardrobe trying to decide what to wear to the theater with the Millers.

Thankfully an adults-only affair.

"And what will you do while we're out? Have Yolande over?"

"No, I need to finish *The Call of the Wild*."

"I'll leave you some vegetable soup and a nice little sandwich. Some potato salad too. How's that?"

"Fine, Mother."

"Or would you prefer egg salad?"

"Either one is fine, Mother, really."

Hours later, certain that her parents were gone, *really* gone, for the evening—that Father hadn't forgotten this or Mother that, Savannah headed to Father's study in the basement.

She had no intention of reading *The Call of the Wild*. She

was dead set on getting her hands on the thing Mother wanted kept from her.

"For heaven's sake, please keep the latest issue of the *Crisis* from her," Savannah had overheard Mother say. "It's all about the war, and Lord knows she has been reading enough about that."

"But the issue celebrates Negro contributions. It may well lift her spirits."

"I doubt that, Wyatt."

"What shall I tell her if she asks about it?"

"Tell her . . . that this month's issue must have been lost in the mail. Or—or, tell her that you let someone at the office borrow it."

"Really, must we lie?"

"Well, then, take it to the office and *make* someone borrow it." After a pause, Mother added, "I do worry about her so."

"She's at that age, darling. Moodiness is to be expected."

"I fear that this is more than moodiness. She barely speaks to us. Claire says she's become quite cold toward Yolande, at moments beastly. The scene at the Sandersons', breaking off with Cary—and you still insist we not bring it all up?"

"It wasn't the end of the world. I say give her time."

"But have you noticed how little she eats?"

"And have you noticed that she is keeping her grades up?"

"Yes, but as I told you when I went to see Garnet about her progress, he said that all the teachers say that lately she only speaks when called upon."

"Please stop worrying, Victoria. It's just a phase. And these have been trying times."

Heading down to the basement, Savannah hoped Father hadn't taken the *Crisis* to the office—he could be forgetful at times.

She searched the drawers of his old-timey oak Chicago C-shape rolltop desk, not far from a corner where Charlie's old baseball bat was propped up against a wall.

"Got it!"

But then, removing the magazine from a bottom desk drawer, Savannah hesitated. Would it drag her into a foul mood? Hadn't she torn up all those articles that had so battered her heart, made her cry? Then she remembered Father saying it was about Negro contributions.

Heading back up, Savannah let her eyes linger on the area where Charlie once had his darkroom, now a storage area for things to donate to the next Association or church bazaar.

In the living room Savannah opened the cabinet of the Edison Amberola, sorted through records—McCormack's "Keep the Home Fires Burning," Caruso's "O Sole Mio," the Original Dixieland Band's "Tiger Rag" . . .

Nah.

She put the records back, stretched out on the davenport with the *Crisis*.

The man on the cover, starch-stiff in uniform, jackboots and all, looked like nothing in the world could keep him from a goal.

Past the table of contents, past ads for Wilberforce, Cheyney, Atlanta University, Morehouse, Knoxville College, Wiley, Florida A&M, Clark . . . Savannah made a mental note to ask Charlie about colleges in New York City the next time she wrote or spoke to him.

On she flipped past Dr. Du Bois's editorial, past a poem, past one article, another. She halted at the Men of the Month column. All soldiers. Dr. Urbane F. Bass of Fredericksburg, Virginia. Lieutenant Mallalieu W. Rush of Atlanta. Captain Napoleon B. Marshall . . .

Did any of them ever open a comfort kit I packed, use a bandage I rolled, put on socks I knitted?

When Savannah reached "LYNCHING RECORD FOR THE YEAR 1918," she started to skip it.

But couldn't.

"According to The Crisis records there were 64 Negroes, 5 of whom were Negro women, and four white men, lynched in the United States during the year 1918, as compared with 224 persons lynched and killed by mob violence during 1917, 44 of whom were lynchings of Negroes. The record for 1918 follows. . . ."

A revolting miasma of dates, places, names.

Of a Sam Edwards in Hazlehurst, Mississippi, burned to death, charged with the murder of a seventeen-year-old white girl . . . Of a Jim Hudson in Benton, Louisiana, hanged for living with a white woman . . . In Collinsville, Illinois, a Robert P. Praeger, white, hanged for making disloyal remarks.

Praeger, Savannah thought. *German, I bet.*

"June 4—Huntsville, Tex., Sarah Cabiness and her six children: George, Peter, Cute, Tenola, Thomas and Bessie, shot: alleged threat by George Cabiness to A.P.W. Allen . . . August 7—Bastrop, La., 'Bubber' Hall, hanged; alleged attack on a white woman. . . ."

Yes, thank goodness we live in the capital.

Savannah couldn't imagine living farther South. Mother had grown up in Charleston, South Carolina, raised by a wealthy aunt after her parents died of scarlet fever. Savannah wondered if Mother spoke so little of her childhood because she had seen Negroes hanged, burned. Maybe growing up in the Southland is what made her so cautious, quick to worry.

Unlike Father. Ease and freedom in his ways. Walk, talk. His luminous laugh. If that's what growing up in New York City did to a person, then yes, New York City was where Savannah wanted to be! Ice-skating on frozen rivers, baseball games . . . Such were the things Father talked about when remembering himself young.

Savannah had splinters of memories of Mother mentioning a Miss Abby, a Ma Clara, she-crabs, a place called Shad Island. Snatches overheard when Mother visited, with her in tow, that strange lady who lived in a top-floor apartment not far from them.

Savannah searched her brain. *Dinah?* Was that her name? Brown-skinned woman. Something wrong with one arm and thick, thick glasses. Mother brought her groceries, packages.

And Mother broke down in their vestibule one day. Arms

around Father's neck, she said, "Thank you, Wyatt. Thank you!"

Father patted her back. "No thanks needed. She has no one but you now. We can well afford to take care of her and this is what we shall do."

"When will we see that lady again?" Savannah had asked when older. The visits had stopped. "The one you give groceries and things."

"Oh, my darling girl, sadly she has passed."

"What was her name again?"

Skimming the "Horizon" column, Savannah zeroed in on mention of Private Harry Thomas, of Philadelphia, a member of the 369th Infantry. The French had decorated him for bravery.

Savannah left the magazine, went upstairs, returned to the living room with Charlie's most recent send. Was Private Harry Thomas of Philadelphia in this breathtaking photograph?

Dear Sis,

Here's one I took of the grand parade here on February 17 in honor of the 369th Infantry. This is the regiment the French called "Men of Bronze" and the Germans the "Hell Fighters." Of the two, "Hell Fighters" is the one that has really caught on.

I covered the parade from the start at 23rd Street and Fifth Avenue. What a jam of humanity with American flags flying, "Welcome Home!" banners, and red-white-and-blue confetti falling like snow. And how the crowds roared when they marched up Lenox Avenue starting at 110th Street in Harlem.

Our Hell Fighters deserve ten parades! They fought their way from the Champagne to the Forest of Argonne and gave battle to and beat the best that the Boche had to offer. Men who left home with Jim Crow on the throne and came back to it with nothing changed.

Yet, how our dusky heroes marched with the air of victors, with heads erect, with eyes front in true soldier fashion. They marched with a jaunty step behind Lieut. Jim Europe's smashing jazz band, a step that thrilled the thousands of spectators along curbs, in doorways, in windows, on rooftops—crowds that cheered, yelled their lungs out, huzzahed. Schools in Harlem closed so the kiddies could attend the parade.

Love to Mother and Father and 10 hugs to you!

Savannah was still staring at the Hell Fighters when she heard a rap on the back door.

KITCHEN CLOCK TICK-TOCKED

Evening, Miss Riddle."

"Evening, Nella."

Nutmeg Nella, tall and slender, had filled in for her mother before, but Savannah had never paid her much attention, like the kids at Dunbar whose fathers were messengers at some government agency or shoemakers, whose mothers were secretaries, seamstresses.

Nella rested her Boston bag on the floor, hung her broadcloth coat on the peg beside the back door, tucked her tam into a coat pocket, and then, with her bag once again in hand, made a beeline for the utility room off the kitchen.

Lickety-split, she was back.

Oxford lace-up pumps traded in for moccasins.

Handkerchief around her head.

Apron over a washed-out blue polka-dot dress.

With bucket and mop in one hand, cleaning caddy in the other, Nella hurried from the kitchen. "I will start up top." She flashed a quick smile.

In the wake of whirlwind Nella, Savannah couldn't think

of anything to do but return to the living room, to the davenport, to the *Crisis*.

Skimmed more ads: 15 phonograph records for $1 . . . books by Kelly Miller, by Carter G. Woodson . . . Lula Robinson Jones Soprano Available for Concerts . . . "Spend your Vacation at Beautiful Idlewild the most wonderfully ideal spot . . ."

Father had toyed with buying property in Idlewild. Just as an investment, he'd said over dinner one evening.

"So we can't ever spend time there?" Savannah had asked.

"Maybe now and then," Father had replied.

"Is it as lovely as Highland Beach?"

That was when Savannah really loved Highland Beach, used to relish Mother's ritual.

With suitcases and hampers unpacked, with the airing out of the cottage begun, they made the pilgrimage to a sacred house. There Mother told of how when his youngest son decided to create a resort for Negroes, the honorable Frederick Douglass was his first investor, how the great man himself designed his own cottage, calling it Twin Oaks.

Mother pointed to the odd narrow second-story balcony of the hip-roofed Queen Anne cottage. "He wanted a view of the Eastern Shore where he was born a slave."

And Mother never tired of telling about the first time she met the Honorable Frederick Douglass, how nervous she was.

Then Savannah thought back to last summer at Highland Beach, her deeper fascination with Twin Oaks. Sketching it over and over, from the front, right side, left side. In one she had even put Douglass on that odd second-story balcony, imagining had he lived to see his cottage completed, what would have gone through his mind as he looked out over Chesapeake Bay.

Freedom.

Sketch Twin Oaks. Walks in the woods. That's all she had wanted to do, but after a few talkings-to from Mother—about *shoulds* and *oughts* and *musts*—she had played the piano when asked, joined in badminton games, charades, had been part of the crew that collected stones and wood for clambakes.

On that last night, with Yolande cracking open lobsters, slurping down clams, she nibbled on corn, a shrimp or two, then when Cary Sanderson beckoned her to join him for a stroll along the beach she felt so ashamed of ever having set her cap at him. But still, beneath banks of gauzy clouds drifting away from a fading sun, she went for that stroll, still she accepted that sterling silver friendship ring.

Savannah glanced at the ad in the *Crisis* for busts of Booker T. Washington, Frederick Douglass, Paul Laurence Dunbar, Bishop Richard Allen: $1.50 each or all four for $5.00. She looked up at the floor-to-ceiling bookcase opposite the davenport. Dunbar, Washington, and Allen looked down on her from the middle shelf. Douglass, looking a bit cross, had pride of place on the nearby fireplace mantel.

Then came the ad that made Savannah smile.

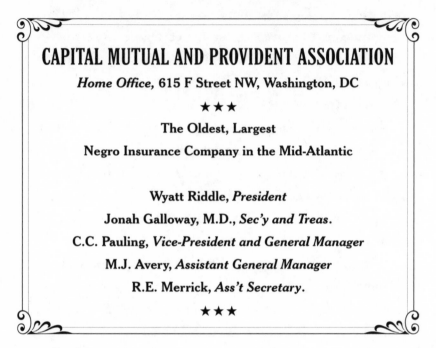

CAPITAL MUTUAL AND PROVIDENT ASSOCIATION

Home Office, 615 F Street NW, Washington, DC

★ ★ ★

The Oldest, Largest

Negro Insurance Company in the Mid-Atlantic

Wyatt Riddle, *President*

Jonah Galloway, M.D., *Sec'y and Treas.*

C.C. Pauling, *Vice-President and General Manager*

M.J. Avery, *Assistant General Manager*

R.E. Merrick, *Ass't Secretary.*

★ ★ ★

That was *her* work, when Father wanted something more modern.

"Think you can help me out, pumpkin?"

"Really?"

"Why not give it a shot?"

She had truly labored over that design. Going back and forth on whether or not to include a photograph or a sketch of the F Street building.

Now, the more she stared at the ad, the more that smile faded. It had always been about *Charlie.* Never her.

Sure, she could design an ad, tidy Father's desk, but . . . Even after Charlie left. Never *her*.

How galling, too, that Charlie was named after Mother's hometown but she got stuck with Savannah.

"So neither of you have any family there?"

"No," Mother had replied.

"Any relatives named Savannah?"

Another no.

"Then why did you name me Savannah?"

"I just love the sound of it," Mother had replied, then mysteriously misted up.

Nella was in the kitchen humming "Hail, Hail, the Gang's All Here."

The scent of Lysol F&F wafted into the living room.

Savannah made up her mind to do something Mother would likely consider a *shouldn't*. Not that Mother ever barked orders at Miss Gertie, treated her in any way unkind. Mother simply kept a polite distance just as she did with Miss Myra, who took in their laundry once a week.

I need to widen my world! Savannah rose from the davenport.

She was almost in the kitchen when—

What do I say?

Savannah spun around, returned to the living room for the Hell Fighters. Fortified, she headed once again for the kitchen.

She stopped at the threshold.

The floor was wet.

The Lysol F&F overwhelming.

Mother had instructed Miss Gertie to not dilute it as much as the manufacturer recommended. She insisted on the same even after Spanish flu waned. And she still had them using Lysol toilet soap, and Father, Lysol shaving cream when he wanted to go back to Colgate's.

≈⌇≈

Nella had scoured, washed, polished, swept. She was just about done mopping, working her way to the back.

Glass cabinet doors . . . porcelain sink . . . white enamel refrigerator . . . porcelain cabriole-legged stove . . . the copper kettle—the whole room gleamed. Drain board and counter-tops clear except for the space beneath one cabinet where Mother kept the stair-step blue willow canisters: **FLOUR, SUGAR, COFFEE, TEA.**

"It feels as if it could rain tonight," Savannah finally said.

Nella kept mopping. "Quite possible."

"May it hold off until you get home."

"Yes, that would be good."

Savannah fiddled with the Hell Fighters. "Did you hear that the NAACP has gotten that man out of jail, the one in South Carolina?"

"The one they said shot off the white man's head?"

"Yes. And isn't it wonderful that the Anthony amendment has been introduced again in the Senate?"

"True, but the clock is ticking fast. Congress is only in session a few more days."

"It's ridiculous. In more than a dozen states women can vote in all elections. In a bunch of others they can vote in some. After what so many women did for the war effort, working in factories, with the Red Cross, the Army Nurse Corps, navy, coast guard, marines, even . . ."

By then Nella had the bucket and mop by the back door. She sighed, wiped her brow.

"Are you all right?" Savannah asked.

"Oh, I'm fine. Just tired. Long day."

"What's wrong with your mother—if you don't mind my asking?"

"Dizzy spells since early morning."

"Has a doctor been to see her?"

"Not yet. Doctors cost money. We're praying it's nothing serious, hoping she'll soon be right as rain."

More fiddling with the Hell Fighters. "So when you aren't filling in for your mother, you clean for other people?"

Nella looked at her blankly.

"I don't mean to intrude or—"

"No intrusion. Just surprised you ask, that's all, Miss Riddle."

Miss Riddle. That sounded so *wrong.* Nella had to be three, four years older. "Just Savannah is fine, Nella."

"I'm not so sure, Miss Riddle."

"I insist."

"Do your parents?"

Savannah decided not to push it.

Nella surveyed the floor. "Since you ask, Miss Riddle, I work some days at Nannie Burroughs's school."

Savannah thought for a bit. "Over on . . ."

"In Lincoln Heights."

"It's for wayward girls?"

"Why, no, Miss Riddle!" Nella looked downright offended. "Nannie Burroughs only accepts girls of good character. No deviants."

"It's a trade school?"

Now Nella looked a wee bit annoyed. "Yes, but it's more than that. As Principal Burroughs is always telling people, she is training young women not to be *servants* but to be of *service*. Most of all to be self-sufficient. Her vision of true womanhood is not of young ladies holding their breaths for Prince Charmings."

Savannah lit up inside.

"She has nothing against marriage per se, but to her mind true womanhood is about a woman being able to *do* for self, *think* for self. Principal Burroughs says, if you're going to be a seamstress be an *expert* at it—so good that you can command top dollar, have your own enterprise even."

Savannah had no interest in being a seamstress or anything like that, but this Nannie Burroughs sure sounded like someone she'd love to meet. "And how many days a week do you clean there?"

"I don't clean there, Miss Riddle. I help out as an instructor in the domestic science department. Teacher's assistant. Normally, Miss Burroughs only hires college graduates, but for some reason she made an exception for me. I'm sure it helps that I go to Miner part-time."

"Oh, so you want to be a teacher?"

"Indeed I do."

"Domestic science?"

"Actually, Miss Riddle, I want to be an English teacher. Above all else I love literature."

Literature? Savannah kicked herself for being surprised by that.

Nella pulled a rag from her apron pocket, rubbed at a spot on the floor. "And just last week I became a qualified Poro agent." That smile again.

Savannah stared at the floor. *Dry, darn it, dry!* She wanted to make tea, have Nella sit across from her at the table, engage in some real conversation, show her the Hell Fighters.

She checked the kitchen clock. "Nella, have you had dinner?"

"Not yet."

Savannah eyed the pot of soup on the stove, thought of the sandwich and either potato or egg salad in the refrigerator. "I'll fix that as soon as the floor dries!"

"That's mighty nice of you, Miss Riddle."

The kitchen clock tick-tocked, tick-tocked.

"All dry!" Savannah said. This was after more tick-tocking from that clock.

"All except for a spot underneath the table," replied a squinting Nella.

Savannah headed over to Nella, handed her the Hell Fighters. "It's one my brother took of the big parade in New York."

"Nice," said Nella.

"You can hold it."

Nella wiped her hands on her apron before taking the photograph.

"Now you just have a sit-down," said Savannah. "I'll prepare you something to eat." Savannah turned on the burner beneath the pot of soup, brought out from the refrigerator a salad plate with a potted ham sandwich and—

Two small bowls.

Mother had made both potato salad and egg salad.

"No, not here, Miss Riddle. I'll take it home, thank you."

"Are you sure?"

Within seconds Nella was at a drawer of kitchen sundries, had a thermos out, a nickel food box too.

Food packed up to go, Nella washed and dried, put things away. "Mummy will bring back your food containers when she comes next week." Nella spirited away to the utility room with mop and bucket.

"So much for widening my world," muttered Savannah.

She was about to give up, return to the davenport, when she was startled by a knock at the back door.

Tick tock. Tick tock. Tick tock.

Another knock.

Like a cautious cat, Savannah tiptoed, peered through the space between the lace café curtains.

There stood a lanky man sporting a fisherman's cap and with his hands shoved in the pockets of a peacoat.

"Yes, may I help you?"

"I come for Nella."

Savannah paused. "Nella, you say?"

"Yes."

"Nella!" Savannah called out.

Water was running.

"Nella!" Savannah called out again louder.

"Coming, Miss Riddle."

Savannah turned, lowered her voice. "There's a man outside asking for you."

"Oh, that's my cousin Lloyd. Come to collect me."

Savannah opened the door. "Please come in."

There was a hint of scorn—or perhaps impatience—on the young man's face when he entered cap in hand.

Blue black.

And possessed of a panther's gaze.

"Miss Riddle, this is my cousin Lloyd. He's recently arrived."

Maybe eighteen, nineteen.

"Lloyd, this is Miss Savannah Riddle."

Savannah extended her hand. "Pleased to meet you."

The young man nodded, turned to Nella. "You ready?"

His accent was much stronger than Nella's, as strong as Miss Gertie's.

"In a jiffy," said Nella. "Just need to wipe down the sink and change."

With Nella gone from the kitchen, Savannah was at wit's end as to what to do. "Would you like a cup of tea or—"

The young man shook his head.

"Would you care to sit down while you wait?"

Again he shook his head.

Savannah glanced at the thermos, the nickel food box on the counter. "That's for Nella, as she hasn't had any dinner. I can make you a sandwich."

With pursed lips, yet again the young man shook his head. "And I don't tink Nella really need wunna food."

Such disdain in his tone, in his eyes.

Thank goodness Nella was soon back and donning her coat, her tam. "Ready!" She reached for her food.

Her cousin tugged her arm. "I let she know we don't need her food."

The frown on Nella's face was a first.

"We got food home," added Lloyd.

"Good night, Miss Riddle."

"Good night, Nella. Good night, Lloyd."

They were almost through the door when Nella turned

around, pulled a piece of paper from her handbag. "A Poro price list. I'd appreciate it if you would pass it on to your kind mother."

Savannah hurried to the door after it closed, peered out. She couldn't hear what they were saying, but she could tell that Nella and her rude cousin were bickering.

Who is he to tell her what food she can and cannot take? It's not as if I was offering them scraps I'd give a dog.

Back at the kitchen table Savannah picked up the photograph, put it, along with the Poro price list, into her pocket, then dealt with what should have been Nella's dinner had it not been for that horrible cousin of hers.

Once satisfied that the kitchen looked as Nella would have left it, Savannah flicked off the lights.

Minutes later—pillows on the davenport fluffed, door to the Edison Amberola shut tight, *Crisis* back in Father's old-timey desk—Savannah was up in her room skimming the Poro price list.

Hair Grower .... 50¢
Liquid Shampoo .... 50¢
Cold Cream .... 21¢
Face Powder .... 19¢
   (Shades: Poro Brown, Dark Brown, Brown, Medium
   Brown, Light Brown, Brunette, Flesh, White)

1 Stem Braid $2.00
Set of Side Curls $2.00
Wigs $25.00

She goes to school. She cleans houses sometimes. She teaches. She sells Poro products.

And she's so cheerful!

What's my excuse?

BEST DAY EVER!

Yolande couldn't believe it!

Was her friend really *back*?

Savannah actually said more than four words to her as they walked behind their parents en route to Metropolitan AME.

Savannah was possessed of such a pleasant air.

Chipper even.

The real shocker came after Sunday service, after people spilled out of the looming redbrick church, after the Riddles and the Holloways gathered around a dormant elm.

"We are thinking of an early dinner at Dade's," said Mr. Riddle. "What do you girls think?"

Yolande's heart sank when Savannah tilted her head to the side, scrunched up her face.

"How about . . . ?"

How about what? Yolande panicked. *How about we just go home? How about you all go without me? How about . . . ?*

"How about you all go to Dade's," Savannah finally said, "and Yolande and I take dinner at Gaskins'?"

Yolande looked at her parents, then at Savannah's. All four seemed as stunned as she was.

"Wouldn't you two prefer Dade's?" asked Mrs. Riddle. "They have those—"

The fathers were handing their daughters fifty-cent pieces by then.

Best day ever! Best day ever!

When they reached Dade's Palace Cafe the girls waved to their parents, walked on.

Yolande felt all tingly.

Then like Christmas Day when Savannah linked arms with her.

And a miracle came.

"Yolande, I know I've been beastly lately. And I just want to say that I'm sorry for being so . . . so, well, so beastly. I hope you can forgive."

Best day ever!

THE SCENT OF LYSOL F&F

Miss Gertie wasn't right as rain the following week. Nella came again, only this time on Sunday afternoon.

Savannah had just changed out of her church clothes when Nella knocked. She too had just come from church it seemed.

Boxy black walking suit.

White batiste blouse.

Plain felt hat.

From the cut of the suit Savannah reckoned it four, five years old. Nella's calfskin-and-serge button-up boots looked a lot like a pair Mother once had. Just like the braided leather handbag.

The night before, Savannah had cleaned her bedroom, bathroom, had even mopped the hallway outside her room. She had also given the room down the hall, a guest room that used to be Charlie's, the once-over. All so that Nella would have less to do.

Idling in the living room, Savannah waited for the scent of Lysol F&F to wend its way in, waited for the kitchen floor to dry. Then she made her move.

"Nella," she called out, heading for the utility room.

"Yes, Miss Riddle?" Nella had changed back into her church clothes. Just two buttons on her jacket left undone.

"I'd like to ask you something."

"Yes, Miss Riddle?"

"Think Nannie Burroughs could use my help?"

"Help with what?"

"The school. Maybe on Saturdays I could stop by and—I don't know, pitch in somehow."

Nella shrugged. "Can't hurt to ask." She glanced at her wristwatch.

"Am I keeping you from something?"

"I do need to get home to Mummy."

"How selfish of me. How about I walk with you some?"

"If you wish, Miss Riddle."

"Just let me grab a coat."

HORRIFIED

Perched in her living room's bay window, Yolande trembled.

What is Savannah thinking?

Walking down the street with a *cleaner*—and a monkey-chasing, tree-climbing one at that!

Yolande was horrified.

BEFORE THE OPEN EYE SALOON

Savannah peppered Nella with questions every step of the way.

When did the school open?

How many students?

Is there a streetcar to Lincoln Heights?

Does the school offer French? Latin?

A challenge.

A passion.

Purpose.

Get engaged.

Take hold of life.

Stop being a mere observer.

"So please do ask Miss Burroughs if she could use me, my help," said Savannah.

"Perhaps you should ask her yourself, Miss Riddle."

Spent of questions, for the first time in a long while Savannah took in her surroundings.

Drab row houses. No turrets, bay windows, balconies.

Next up, a cram of shops with weatherbeaten signs. Barrows's Meat Market had pieces of paper stuck askew at dirty windows—Fresh Hams 25¢ lb. . . . Pork Loin 25¢ lb. . . .

Affixed to the second-story window, a big sign: ROOMS.

Next door, a secondhand shop with a clutter of tea kettles, milk glass china, nickel silver pitchers and trays, puff boxes, hobnail bowls, carpet sweeper, ash can, clock, candlesticks.

Up ahead, an unsavory-looking fellow leaned against a streetlamp. Cheap baggy suit. Scowl on his face.

Savannah slowed her pace between Bailey's Down Home Cook Shop and Rex's Pool Hall. She made a full stop right before the Open Eye Saloon. Outside, three scruffy boys in worn knickers and dingy shirts were shooting marbles.

"Are you all right, Miss Riddle?" asked Nella.

Savannah swallowed. "It's just that, that—I've taken up enough of your time. Thank you for all the information. You get along to your mother."

"I understand, Miss Riddle."

Out of nowhere a little boy came dancing up to Savannah. "Hello, Miss Fine Lady!"

Savannah recoiled. "Oh, it's—"

The boy thumped his chest. "I name Bim."

"Bim, right." Then to Nella with a weak smile, "Thanks again for your time."

Oblivious to Bim's and Nella's goodbyes, Savannah did an about-face, skittered away, eyes on the ground, wishing for wings. She'd never been that deep into the southwest quadrant, didn't know anybody who lived there, didn't know a soul who lived in a neighborhood like this *anywhere* in the city.

It was blocks and blocks and blocks before she changed her pace to a stroll while chiding herself for being afraid of her own people.

Yolande was still in the window, and fuming, when Savannah turned onto their block.

IN THE WHOLLY IMPOSSIBLE

That fear she'd felt in Southwest spurred Savannah to do better, be stronger, get bolder.

Throwing caution to the wind, the following Saturday she made a step in that direction.

Aware that the ride wouldn't be a short one, when she boarded the streetcar, along with her purse she had a sketch pad.

As she took the first available seat in the front, she could hear Father's commandment: "We must always take full advantage of what we *can* do." The streetcars were one of the few places where there was no color line.

With the rumble and roll of the car, there were honks of horns, clip-clopping of horse-drawn carriages, newsies hawking the *Herald*—

"All Warsaw in darkness!"

"Typhus scourge rages in Russia!"

"Arrested as robber, killed in gun fight!"

So much bad news everywhere. All the time! What a cursed and broken world! thought Savannah amid the babble and chatter of a clutch of cyclists, of people crowding sidewalks. Some in a stroll. Others in hurry-up mode.

Just yesterday a six-year-old boy died and scores of other people were injured when a bomb went off in a Southside Chicago apartment building. All because the building's occupants were Negroes. And before Savannah left the house that morning, she overheard her parents talking about Wobblies in some Massachusetts town blowing *themselves* up instead of the mill they targeted.

There has never been a time when there wasn't misery in the world somewhere.

Sifting out the street sounds, Savannah fastened onto sad sights right there before her very eyes.

Negro men, white men, in tattered uniforms, some propped up against buildings.

Arm missing.

Leg missing.

Scarred face.

Caps turned up.

"Whatever you can spare!"

"I was at the Battle of Cantigny!"

"I was at Argonne!"

The more aggressive ones, tin cups, upside-down caps in hand, waylaid people waiting to cross a street.

A double amputee sat on a piece of wood with wheels, a cigar box his begging bowl. The grease-stained paperboard around his neck bore a crudely lettered plea: "HEP ME PLEEZE."

Savannah thought about the streams of SITUATION WANTED ads newspapers carried, two cents a word, that began "DISCHARGED SOLDIER."

Wanting a job as a porter.

Kitchen man.

Janitor.

Chauffeur.

Bookkeeper.

Any office position.

Two years college.

Sober.

Handy with tools.

Savannah changed the subject, turned her attention to passengers on the streetcar.

The prim Negro lady near the rear in a plain gray coat and hat with a veil.

Bright-eyed twin boys in matching tweed Dubbelbilt suits.

The odd-looking white man: bulbous nose, chicken lips, dressed like a member of a barbershop quartet.

Savannah settled on sketching the bright-eyed twins. Not as they were but as they could be. In gunny sacks poised for a race in a summer field, crowded with lupines, day lilies, daisies. *Once back home I'll do it over in pastels.*

As the sunlight grew brighter, as a slight sweetness ambled into the bracing March air, Savannah put down her sketch pad, soaked in the sights. Really, the lack thereof.

Fewer homes and buildings, more forest and farmland. More birdsong.

Everyone she saw—walking, driving, riding in a buggy—all Negro. So were the other remaining passengers when the streetcar reached its last stop: the twin boys and that prim lady with a veil.

Up, up, up Savannah walked, the climb exhilarating. At the top she paused, wonderstruck. It was larger than she imagined. Nella hadn't said there were so many buildings. One in the forefront was truly stately, divine. Wraparound porch, three-sided bow windows, gables.

Savannah headed, not for that one, but for the three-story white clapboard, the one that commanded the highest elevation.

From its raised porch hung a white banner emblazoned with bold black words: WE SPECIALIZE IN THE WHOLLY IMPOSSIBLE.

On the porch Savannah patted her hair, shook out her dress. Head up, she entered.

A petite mahogany girl rose from a desk behind the counter. "Good morning. How may I help you?"

French accent.

Savannah stepped forward, smiling. "My name is Savannah Riddle, and I would like to speak with Miss Nannie Burroughs."

"I am sorry, but Principal Burroughs is not here. Perhaps I can help you?"

Savannah suddenly felt undone, stupid even. *Now what?*

"I wanted to know . . ."

"Yes?"

"I wanted to know if the school could use some help?"

"Help?"

"A helping hand. I would love to spend some hours tutoring in—or teaching . . ."

"For that, yes, you must speak with Principal Burroughs."

Savannah's heart sank. "Well, thank you very much."

The black candlestick telephone on the desk made Savannah feel even dumber. *I should have called first. What got into me?*

"Is Nella here by any chance? Nella Walcott?"

"I'm afraid not."

Savannah put on a happy face. "Perhaps some other time."

"Or you could wait if you wish. Principal Burroughs should be back shortly." With a gentle wave of a hand, the girl bid Savannah to take a seat in the lounge.

Savannah headed for the wingback armchair with stout, squat legs, the front ones slendering down to talon-and-ball feet. On the way she picked up a flyer from a golden oak gateleg table with barley twist legs.

At the top:

BEFORE DECIDING WHERE TO ATTEND SCHOOL
Send for Catalogue of
The National Training School for Women & Girls

Savannah skimmed the rest of the flyer.

"The entire future of your daughter depends upon . . . Thousands of untrained women are simply pegging out an existence. Why not become a skilled worker in your line and make something better than a living— make a life."

Make a life. Make a life. Make a life!
Flyer folded up and tucked into her purse, Savannah glanced at magazines fanned out on a table beside that wingback chair. Some her parents subscribed to—the *Crisis*, the *Journal of Negro History*. Others she had never even heard of.

Like the *Crusader.* Its motto "Onward for Democracy . . . Upward for the Race."

A young woman on every cover.

October 1918: a Dutch bob and readiness in her eyes.

November 1918: flowing locks, sunbeam smile.

February 1919: neat sweater and skirt, spat pumps, atop a

stool, telephone in hand, looking like she knows everything there is to know.

Each young woman was clearly doing more than pegging out an existence. So fearless.

When Savannah saw that the magazine was out of New York City—2299 Seventh Avenue—she wondered how far that was from Charlie, then returned to the issue with the young woman sporting a Dutch bob.

Who is she? Where does she live? What does she do?

Savannah was just about to flip through to find out when the front door opened.

Along with a gust of wind, an even more fearless-looking woman with lustrous dark chocolate skin strode in—and so smartly dressed in a green gabardine dress beneath a black walking coat. On her head, a fanciful black satin-and-tulle cartwheel hat at a jaunty angle.

This has to be her.

Savannah rose, not sure if she should approach or wait to be summoned.

"Principal Burroughs," said the girl behind the counter. "This young lady is here to see you."

Approach.

Savannah hurried over.

"Good day," said Nannie Burroughs.

"Good day, ma'am."

"And what is it that I can do for you?"

"I—I apologize for just showing up—for not telephoning first—I— Hello, Miss Burroughs, my name is Savannah Riddle and I, I . . ."

Nannie Burroughs squinted. Her smile gave life to dimpled cheeks. "Wyatt and Victoria's daughter?"

Savannah felt somewhat relieved.

Puzzled too.

"Yes, ma'am." She had never heard the woman's name on Mother's or Father's lips.

"And what can I do for you, Miss Savannah Riddle?"

When Savannah finished, Nannie Burroughs seemed somewhat stunned. Slightly reared back on her heels, she said, "You really want to pitch in at *my* school?"

"Yes, ma'am," replied Savannah, eyes trained on that bedazzling cartwheel hat.

"Why?"

"Because, well, Nella—Nella Walcott told me about how wonderful—"

"And how do you know Nella?"

"Her mother, she cleans for us and she fell ill and so Nella filled in for her. And we got to talking and . . ." Savannah ran out of words.

Nannie Burroughs removed one black calfskin glove, the other. "How about you have a tour first," she said.

"I'd be happy to show her around," said the girl behind

the counter. She grabbed a wrap from a peg. Reaching Savannah, she extended her hand. "Mona Auguste.

"This is Pioneer Hall," said Mona as she and Savannah headed for the door. "I'll tell you more about it upon our return."

The house a few yards from Pioneer Hall, the stately, divine one, was the Mary G. Burdette model home.

"It is where those on the domestic science course practice. One week a student is a chambermaid, the next a parlor maid, cook, or head housekeeper. After several rotations every girl is an expert in every job. Our model home also doubles as our visitors' lodge and is available for banquets."

A few steps on was the Maggie L. Walker Hall—

"Dormitories and classrooms."

Then Whitfield Hall—

"Dormitories and recreation room. Also it's where music lessons are held."

"Oh, I play the piano. Perhaps I can teach girls to play."

Mona merely smiled.

Alpha Hall—more dormitories and classrooms.

A single-story long building needed no explanation because there were signs above its three doors.

LAUNDRY.

PRINTERY.

CLASSROOM.

Next, the community service building, home to a library and a shop.

"Our library is open to the public," Mona explained. "As for the store, along with general dry goods we sell cakes, pies, and other baked goods students make."

In addition to that, the students planted gardens in the spring and in the summer ran a farm stand down the hill.

Principal Burroughs's gospel of self-sufficiency was so real.

"There are our teachers, of course, but other than them and a man or two who comes in the spring to plow up for our garden and do heavy repairs, we run the place ourselves."

Before each building, beds of tulips, crocuses, hyacinth, daffodils, freesia poised to burst into bloom.

Just like Savannah.

A place with such purpose. She could *feel* it.

Girls solo, in groups, in wash dresses and shoes with Cuban heels, walked swiftly, regally in and out of buildings. Some twelve or so. Others maybe eighteen or older. And they all seemed so happy.

"Just last week a group painted the parlor in the model home." Savannah and Mona were heading back to Pioneer Hall. "The domestic science girls prepare all our meals and do the shopping. Those in dressmaking and millinery make most of our clothes, those in hairdressing do our hair, and once a week we get manicures from girls studying manicure and massage."

They passed a trio of floppy ginkgo trees.

"And you, Savannah, where do you attend school?"

"Dunbar."

"That is where Principal Burroughs went—back when it was the M Street School, of course. Graduated with honors."

Savannah had been past proud years back when one of Uncle Madison's photos appeared in a *Crisis* article on old M Street School opening on N Street as Dunbar. The *Crisis* had hailed Dunbar as the "Greatest Negro High School in the World."

When Savannah and her parents, Yolande and hers, first toured the soaring brick and stone-trimmed building—a castle!—that had *everything*, from a swimming pool to a fifteen-hundred-seat auditorium, Savannah was panicky, fearing that she'd never find her way around, would get lost, swallowed up in that huge school.

But, oh, how absolutely ecstatic she and Yolande had been that their walk to, from school would be a whole five minutes longer.

Now Dunbar no longer loomed so large, their twenty-minute walk to, from a bore.

As she and Mona entered Pioneer Hall, Savannah thought maybe she could persuade Yolande to join her in helping out at Nannie Burroughs's school—if, that is, the woman first said yes to her.

Sisters!

Maybe she and Yolande could have that again.

Tour of Pioneer Hall completed, Mona took Savannah to
Principal Burroughs's office.

"And how do you find us?"

"It is grand, Miss Burroughs. What a wondrous thing you
have built! Just marvelous!"

"We try," said Burroughs with a wink, a sassy smile.

"So do you think I might—"

"I think we just might be able to use your helping hands.
On one condition."

"And that is, Miss Burroughs?"

"Written permission from your parents."

SPIRALING BLUE LEAVES

Head up, like her nerve.

"I have an announcement!"

She had decided to go on the offense. Tell. Not ask.

"And it is . . . ?" That was Father.

Savannah had just helped herself to peas. He had just passed the parsley new potatoes and looked longingly at the T-bone steak on his plate.

Savannah cleared her throat. "I'm keen to pitch in at Nannie Burroughs's school on Saturdays."

Father, Mother looked at each other.

Then at her.

As if she'd said she wanted to join a circus or marry a chinchilla coat–wearing, gold-toothed gangster.

"Have you lost your mind?" Mother looked horrified.

"Where did this come from?" asked Father.

"I want to be useful. I can tutor girls in English or French or some other subject. They have a newsletter. I can help out with that. I can teach piano."

"What do you even know about that school?" Mother again.

"Nella told me about it. She works there part-time. The other day—"

"That's absurd," snapped Mother. "Now please help yourself to potatoes so that we can get on with dinner."

Savannah plopped a spoonful of parsley new potatoes onto her plate.

"Now you may say grace," commanded Mother.

If making a self-portrait, Savannah would have drawn steam, spouting, spewing from her ears, the words DON'T IGNORE ME! ballooning from her head.

"Wyatt, we received a postcard from the Blakes."

"Where are they again?"

"Denver."

"Their grandchild? Has he or she arrived?"

"Not as of the mailing of the card."

Savannah barged in. "Is that it? No discussion?"

"About what?" asked Father. "The Blakes?"

"No, about *me* and Nannie Burroughs's school."

"Not at this time, pumpkin."

"Why not?"

"You know how I can get if my steak goes cold." Father gave her that smile of his that always made her melt.

Not this time. "Well, one day *you* two are going find out how I can get if—"

From Father a withering look.

"I'm seventeen, not *seven*," she mumbled, then speared a potato.

Savannah looked around at the dining room with its burl and marquetry china cabinet, buffet, sideboard, and all the rest. Such heavy furniture. Dark.

She glared at the vase of flowers in the center of the table, flanked by Mother's precious Tiffany candlesticks with off-white tapers.

It's not as if we don't have electricity.

Near Father, Mother's precious Tiffany salt and pepper cellars with their silly little spoons. Too tiny for Father's hands. *Why can't she just have salt and pepper shakers? Doesn't Tiffany's make them?* Savannah hated it all.

The wallpaper—tiny rose and pale yellow flowers on a background of spiraling blue leaves. *There are no blue leaves in nature.*

From where she sat she could see some of the parlor and decided to hate everything in that room too.

Blue velvet settee and chairs.

Silly-looking little footstool.

Marble turtle-top tables.

Another pair of dumb Tiffany candlesticks on the fire-place mantel.

Same wallpaper with those ridiculous blue leaves.

And Mother's pride and joy—the crystal chandelier and matching floor lamps.

The room is a mausoleum. Only ever used when there was a

dinner party or when some very important person visited, and yet spring and summer Mother kept the room in flowers.

What a waste!

Savannah picked at peas on her plate. She hadn't touched her steak. She pushed her plate away.

"Can you give me one good reason?"

"Savannah, please," chided Mother. After a few bites she added, "For one, that school is all the way out in Lincoln Heights."

"But a streetcar goes out there."

"And you know this how?" asked Mother.

"I can read maps." Savannah thought she'd leave it there but then decided *no!* "I went there today."

Savannah looked Mother dead in the face, unblinking.

Father's knife, fork, hit his plate.

Mother stopped chewing, swallowed.

"You did what?" Father's voice was like coming thunder.

Savannah lowered her head, her grip on boldness slipping away.

Mother's silverware was now on her plate too. "You *told* us that you were going out to sketch and that you might take in a photoplay later with Yolande."

"I did sketch. On the cars. As for Yolande . . ."

Father's eyes narrowed. "So you flat-out lied to us?"

Silence.

Out of the corner of her eye Savannah saw Father rubbing his chin.

"I'm disappointed in you, Savannah. Very disappointed."

"But I *did* sketch. On the cars."

"Anything short of the truth is a lie, and you know that, Savannah."

She heard not only anger in Father's voice. There was hurt too.

"I knew that if I told you, you'd probably say no. I thought that if I went there first, saw that it was a good place for myself—and it is. It really is. As far as I could tell, people in the surrounding area are Negro. The school is only a short walk from the streetcar stop. The girl who gave me a tour said that the only time any men are on the premises is in the spring."

Silence.

"Nannie is—"

"You know her?"

"Yes, of course. She is a member of the Association."

"Really?"

Whenever Mother hosted an Association tea or luncheon, Mary Church Terrell was there, Mattie Bowen, Emma Merritt. She ticked off more names in her head. But never Nannie Burroughs.

"Savannah." The ferocity in Father's voice was gone. "Your mother and I will discuss this later and let you know."

"I am sorry, Wyatt, but I do not think that there is anything to discuss. She simply *cannot* go traipsing off to Lincoln Heights."

Savannah threw her napkin onto the table, shot up.

"Savannah!"

That was Father.

"Sit back down, young lady."

Savannah slumped into her chair.

"Sit up straight and finish your dinner," Mother said calmly.

"I've lost my appetite."

Father weighed in. "Then take a few minutes to *find* it."

Savannah picked at more peas, then cut into her cold T-bone steak. "It's just not fair," she muttered. "Father, you go out to the reform school once a month to counsel boys. And, Mother, years ago didn't you have a club, one that helped poor women with children?"

"Yes, I did. The Mothers' Helpers Club."

"What, did you just *abandon* those poor people?"

"Tone, young lady," said Father. "Tone."

"No, I did not abandon those people. When the Association formed, the Mothers' Helpers Club was folded into it. Part of the point of the Association was to pool resources and not duplicate efforts. Younger hands are now at the helm of what became of my club."

Savannah pressed on. "And when the Association sprang into action to help save Frederick Douglass's estate, you drafted letter after letter soliciting funds to pay off the mortgage. And you've spent hours on restoration plans. You even pitched in and pulled weeds and got rid of trash. And look at the work you do around the Anthony amendment. You two are always supporting all kinds of things."

"And your point?" Mother's voice possessed a lot more bite.

"You both have your causes. Why can't I have a cause?"

"The Bethel Junior Literary Society awaits you."

"With all due respect, Mother, sitting around with members of the smart set having debates and giving speeches on the latest books read is hardly a cause."

"What about your school's newspaper?" asked Father.

"I've given that up."

"Really? When? Why?"

Mother cleared her throat.

"What?"

"Father, Cary is the editor. Things would be, you know, a bit awkward."

"Oh, yes, I see."

"There's the Y," Mother chimed in.

"The war is over. Or hadn't you noticed?"

"Savannah . . ." By then Father had abandoned his steak.

"There is to be a new kind of comfort kit," said Mother. "One for our soldiers unable to find employment."

Savannah thought for a bit. "I can do that some Saturdays and go out to Lincoln Heights other Saturdays."

Mother dabbed her mouth with her napkin.

Savannah speared another parsley potato. "You two are always talking about how I must be a credit to the race, how I must lift as I climb."

"Yes, but—"

"But I can only be a credit in a way *you* see fit. I can only lift in the way *you* think I should."

"We are merely looking out for you."

"No wonder Charlie never comes home! No wonder he wanted to get as far away from you as possible!"

"That's enough!" said Father. "To your room!"

From the tempo, the timbre, she knew whose rap it was.

"Come in, Mother," Savannah said drily from her bed, stretched out on her back, hands beneath her head, eyes fixed on her ceiling fan, shoes kicked off.

Mother perched on the foot of her bed. "My darling girl, please don't be upset with us. Understand that we are just trying to look out for you, protect you, save you from—"

"Protect me, save me from *what*? Nannie Burroughs?" Savannah refused to look at Mother.

"Well, yes, in a way. She is of the more radical element."

"She runs a school. What's so radical about that?"

"Savannah, we live in perilous times, on the razor's edge. You don't know what it was like in the capital before. It was called the colored man's paradise. Negroes prospered in multiples."

"Father is prosperous, so is Yolande's, and the Lees, the Sandersons, the—"

"It was even more so in the past. Barber shops that catered to prominent white men owned by Negroes. Hundreds of our people had good government jobs. Then President Wilson came in and drew the color line in civil service. Treasury Department . . . Government Printing Office . . . all the way through. Many of our men with good jobs—some even in supervisory positions—were demoted, others fired. Wilson opened the way to harder treatment of Negroes all over the city."

"But what does all this have to do with Nannie Burroughs's school?"

"It's so far away, for one. And you won't be around anyone you know."

"But I told you Nella works there part-time."

"I mean people you've spent time with. People like Yolande."

"You mean our kind of people?"

"No, I'm not saying that. Not at all."

"Is Nannie Burroughs not our kind of people, Mother? Is that it?"

"No, I'm not saying that!"

"Then what's the harm, Mother?"

Mother had that weepy look. Savannah knew what was coming.

"I know, Mother, I know. I know how after Charlie the doctor said you would probably never be able to have another child. I know how you prayed and prayed, how much you especially wanted at least one daughter. How the years passed and passed and you kept praying and praying and praying."

You are my miracle, Savannah remembered Mother saying when she was very young, when they were out for a stroll, when Mother washed her hair, tucked her into bed.

How alarmed Mother got over a skinned knee, a cold. When Spanish flu hit, Mother was in such a panic. All that Lysol F&F.

And those stupid dress rehearsals for the first time she

and Yolande were allowed to leave their block. Mother had actually made a map of the route they were to take to Board's. *Three times* they practiced the route.

Mother walking a few feet behind them.

Mother reminding them to look both ways.

Mother had moved to the window. "Things are becoming more dangerous for us, Savannah. With the war over, so many soldiers unable to find work . . ." Mother was wringing her hands. "With these being hard times for so many people, whitefolks are getting their backs up more and more, grumbling. The mere sight of a Negro in uniform . . . And what with so many of our people leaving parts South for up North, out West . . . This migration is growing greater and with it, the rage."

"But why?"

"Money. Power. It's always one or the other. Or both. Added to that, there's fear . . . My point, Savannah, is that you seem so keen to just—just shrug off, turn your back on, even, all that we've made possible for you." Mother shook her head, rubbed her upper arms as if she had a chill. "At such a time as this."

Savannah thought for a bit, then returned to her goal. "But, Mother dear, what does any of this have to do with Nannie Burroughs's school?"

A VERY BAD INFLUENCE

Yu're going to do *what*?"

That Nella was a bad, a very bad influence.

Yolande had heard that people from the islands did voodoo, drank blood.

Had Nella cast a spell on Savannah?

"Why would you want to volunteer *there*?"

"You should see it, Yolande! It's a little village, a piece of paradise. Girls out there, they really *do* things!"

"Like what?"

"They have a laundry business, a store. In the summer, a farm stand."

"You want to do laundry, work in a shop, sell vegetables?"

"Girls out at Lincoln Heights *run* things. They are—they are *making lives*."

Yolande shook her head. "And your parents are letting you do this?"

"Yes. Two Saturdays a month—and maybe more. And on two conditions. I must keep my grades up and Father must drive me out there and pick me up at four."

They were a few blocks away from Dunbar. Savannah in a navy blue pleated skirt and shawl-collared white blouse, her tan coat, like her school bag, slung over a shoulder. Yolande in a white tucked-collar blouse beneath a burgundy serge-and-silk ripple-back suit was increasingly annoyed by what seemed to her Savannah's ever-widening strides.

"I've heard very bad things about Nannie Burroughs," Yolande sputtered.

Both girls were walking in white hose and black patent leather Mary Janes.

"Like what?"

"She doesn't much care for our set."

"Nonsense. If that were true she wouldn't have welcomed me to lend a helping hand. And you know she went to M Street. Graduated with honors."

"But she's from common folk. I think her parents or maybe it was her grandparents—in any event she comes from *slaves*. Virginia, I think."

Yolande didn't know what to make of Savannah's queer look.

"So what?" Savannah finally said. "Dr. Woodson's parents were slaves for many years. Ida Wells-Barnett, she was born a slave. She wasn't in slavery for long, but—"

"But—"

"But what? Think about it. If Nannie Burroughs graduated with honors from M Street, if Dr. Woodson graduated from *Harvard*, if Ida Wells-Barnett became a first-rate journalist—what does that tell you? For heaven's sake, Frederick Douglass was born a slave!"

Savannah's mind was moving too fast for Yolande.

"Well, I bet it's a trap!"

"That's so silly."

"I bet Nannie Burroughs wants to trick you into thinking she likes you, only to humiliate you or something. Revenge for what was done to her?"

"*Please*, Yolande."

"You see, after M Street she wanted to teach at one of the schools for us here. Anna Cooper and Mary Church Terrell controlled who got teaching jobs, and they blocked her."

"Why?"

"They wanted the best and brightest."

"But Nannie Burroughs graduated with honors."

Yolande ran a finger across the back of her hand. "By 'brightest' I don't mean in terms of brains."

REVENGE AFTER ALL?

No tutoring anyone in English or in any other subject.

Not assigned to the print shop or to the store.

Nothing like that.

Mona gave her an old dress, an apron, a wrap for her head, a run-down pair of shoes, then introduced her to the crew tasked with making Whitfield Hall spick-and-span.

Savannah's first impulse was to telephone Father, ask him to come for her quick.

Nannie Burroughs's revenge after all?

But then Savannah bucked up. *It's a test. They want to see how sincere I am.*

Polishing furniture. Polishing brass. Washing windows. Bringing mirrors to a shine. Scrubbing. Sweeping. Mopping. Beating rugs.

Savannah had never done this much manual labor in her life. By noon she was bone-tired.

In body.

In spirit, on a cloud. For Nannie Burroughs's school was music without song, a field of dreams.

There were other girls from Haiti like Mona.

Three from Liberia.

From Illinois, Pennsylvania, New York, New Hampshire, Connecticut, Mississippi—there were girls from more than twenty states—with a slew from Virginia.

Kind, friendly, cheery. No one put on airs. Everyone seemed so free within themselves.

Over a lunch of cheese sandwiches and lemonade, Savannah sat dumbfounded, speechless, as Mona talked of opening a school like Nannie Burroughs's in Port-au-Prince, as Martha spoke of doing the same in Monrovia.

The reed-thin Allen twins, Ruth and Ruby, planned to start a janitorial service in Chicago.

Long, tall Blanche Corbin aimed to own a string of beauty shops in Pittsburgh.

"A millinery shop back home," said doll-faced Flossie Hale from Newport News.

"Restaurant!" declared Myrtle from Detroit.

"Missionary!" said Gloria. "To whatever country God calls me."

They were all so geared up to *make a life!* So confident that their destinies were in their hands.

"What about you, Savannah?" asked Mona.

I want to move to New York City, be with Charlie.

Hardly a plan, not compared to being a missionary or owning beauty shops.

"I haven't quite decided," she said sheepishly.

She had to do better than that!

"An artist. I'm thinking of becoming a painter."

Instant regret. *Why did I say that?*

Not bold enough!

Not *doing* enough!

⁓✕⁓

Later, after more brass doorknobs and push plates were polished, more furniture dusted, windows cleaned, floors swept, mopped, after working up a bit of sweat, after sips of more lemonade . . .

When Savannah saw the black Buick pull up, she wished God had called for a long, long pause, wished she could linger longer on the steps of Pioneer Hall gazing out from this high and lofty place.

"Father, can you do me a favor?" she asked as the Buick pulled off.

"Depends."

"Next time can you drop me off down the hill and wait for me down there when you come back to get me?"

MISS TING

The next time Savannah came prepared. She brought her own work clothes, but much to her surprise—

"You can help with getting the newsletter ready for mailing," said Mona.

Stapling. Folding. Stacking. Stapling. Folding. That was more up Savannah's alley. And made all the less tedious with Elza from Taft, Oklahoma, Arabella from Boston, and Rosetta from Wilmington, Delaware, filling her in on doings at the school, from a social the last Friday of every month to Dr. Woodson's monthly lectures.

"Do you play basketball?" asked Rosetta, planting before Savannah another stack to staple and fold.

No, Savannah didn't know how to play basketball. Mother thought she might get hurt.

"No, I've never played. Why do you ask?"

"We have basketball teams."

"Lunch!" That was Mona entering the printery with a picnic basket. Behind her, an Allen twin hugged a large jar of iced tea.

Worktable cleared, Mona doled out sandwiches. "The cups," she said to the Allen twin. "We forgot the cups."

"I'll go fetch them," said the girl.

Mona turned to Savannah. "Then will you take the workman his lunch, please."

A sandwich wrapped in wax paper, a napkin, small thermos.

"He's down by the big garden plot, I think. If he's not there, check behind the store."

He was sawing hard, fast. Thick branches, skinny ones littered the ground.

"Lunch," said Savannah to the back of him.

Bib overalls.

Check shirt.

Dusty work boots.

Chore hat.

"You can rest it there 'pon the stump."

The voice gave Savannah pause, but she shrugged it off, went about placing the lunch on the stump.

She heard the workman climbing down the ladder.

Duty done, Savannah turned to head back—

"Well, well, well." From a pocket he pulled out a handkerchief, wiped his brow.

He seemed taller than when he stood in her kitchen with his rude self.

"Savannah, nuh?"

She had welcomed Nella to call her by her first name. But she didn't like the way it came out of *his* mouth. "Yes, that's my name, Savannah Riddle."

"I'm—"

"Boyd, is it?"

"Lloyd." He looked her up and down. "So how come you here?"

Savannah straightened her back. "I help out here."

He looked her up and down.

Again.

"Help doing what? Fainting and falling down?"

What a cad!

"I can do quite a lot," Savannah shot back. "The first time I was on a cleaning crew. This time I'm helping out with a mailing."

Lloyd leaned the saw against the tree. "Some sorta school assignment?"

"No. It's just something I choose to do."

Lloyd stepped over to the tree stump, sat down on the ground. He took out a pocketknife, wiped it on the napkin, unwrapped the sandwich. "I had a big breakfast." He cut the sandwich in two. "Don't like to eat much while on a job." He put half of the sandwich into the napkin and handed it to Savannah.

Savannah froze. "I have lunch waiting for me in the—"

"Or is it that you scared to break bread with a workingman?"

Savannah snatched the half a sandwich out of his hand. "Of course not." She plopped down beside him.

She would not be cowed by his silence. Nor by his stares. "So when exactly did you come to the capital?"

"Few months back."

"From Barbados?"

He shook his head. "Saint Thomas."

"But I thought—"

"Born in Barbados, but a while back I moved to Saint Thomas."

"What did you do there?"

"This and that on a plantation."

Savannah finished off the sandwich as fast as she could, not chewing nearly as many times as she had been raised to do. "Well, it was nice seeing you again, Lloyd." She rose.

"You too, Miss Ting."

During Savannah's next time at Nannie Burroughs's little village on a hill, she was grabbing at weeds in one of the large, stone-bounded raised beds that dotted the lawn outside Pioneer Hall when she looked up, saw Lloyd striding her way.

Good Lord!

"Still here?" He actually smirked.

"Well, of course I'm still here. When I make a commitment I see it through."

Lloyd snorted. "Miss Ting, if you gine work, put yuh back into it. You ain't doing the earth no good a'tall with yuh weak little jabs." He picked up the trowel beside her, made a deep dig into the dirt. "You want to dig up every root."

"I was going to get to that. I have my own way of doing things."

Lloyd snorted, walked away.

Thank goodness!

Savannah returned to her way of weeding.

But then Lloyd came back.

And with a big ole shovel. He jabbed it into the ground. "Now dig like yuh life depend 'pon it."

"As I said, I have my own way of—"

"Dig, I tell you."

Savannah had never handled a shovel before. In springtime Father always turned the soil over. He did all the major weeding in their backyard garden, in the front yard flower plots too. The most she and Mother did was plant seeds and transplant seedlings they'd grown in the shed.

Savannah grabbed the shovel. With both hands on the handle she stabbed into the ground, then lifted the shovel with too much force.

Dirt went flying.

She went flying, fell back on the ground.

Lloyd roared with laughter.

Savannah's upper lip quivered.

Begrudgingly, she accepted Lloyd's outstretched hand.

He practically yanked her up, snickering.

Savannah shook her dress, brought her braid over her shoulder to pat out any dirt.

"You know, you aren't a very nice person, Lloyd! Hard to believe you and Nella are in the same family."

"You want nice, Miss Ting? You better go back to yuh world of the bourgeoisie. Back to yuh little cocoon."

"Will you stop calling me Miss Ting! You know my name. I'd appreciate it if you would use it!" Savannah stormed off.

"Where you going?"

Savannah kept walking.

Faster when she heard his footfalls.

In just a few strides Lloyd was by her side. "Look, I was only making sport. Come back. Let me show you how to dig." There was no sting, no mockery in his voice.

One foot back.

One foot front.

Front foot on the blade.

"Now lean in a little."

Push down with back straight.

"Give yuh weight to the back leg now. Bend yuh hip and knees."

Lift up the dirt.

"Now you can weed properly," said Lloyd.

Once Savannah had all the earth turned over, she sat down on her haunches, commenced to pull up weeds.

"No, no," said Lloyd. "Take off the gloves."

"But—"

"If you want to do it right you need to get yuh hands dirty."

Lloyd looked around and down, frowned. "You ain't set up properly." He jogged off. "I soon come back," he said over his shoulder.

Poised on the rim of that stone-bounded flower bed, Savannah spotted a pair of blue jays making a nest in a linden tree.

Instinct. All instinct.

Intently she watched the birds sail down to the ground, pick through winter waste—bark, twigs, leaves. Shoving aside some things. Catching up others in their beaks.

Little heads bobbing, twitching.

Taking flight again, returning to the linden to lay, place, make their instinct-driven lace of winter waste.

Savannah rose, gingerly stepped closer to the tree.

Gazing at those jays . . .

If she were drained of, freed from everything she'd been taught at school, at church, from Mother, from Father . . .

If I were just instinct, being—?

Lloyd returned with a rake and a tiller atop a wheelbarrow. It was full of dead, moldy leaves and scraps of skinny branches.

The blue jays let out a series of whirs and whines.

"You need to feed the good earth, stroke her," said Lloyd.

"The girls here smart to save leaves from the fall. So after you weed . . ."

He had just finished with his instructions when Mona appeared.

"I'm sorry, your name again?"

"Lloyd."

"Well, Lloyd, Principal Burroughs would like to see you. She wants an estimate on repairing the toolshed and some fencing."

Lloyd and Mona were long gone when Savannah went back to weeding. A few minutes in, she found that when she grabbed at a weed sometimes all she got was a half handful of dirt, which she then had to shake off. She looked around. With Lloyd nowhere in sight, she removed her gardening gloves. After weeding, she kept the gloves off as she fed the good earth handfuls of mucky leaves and scraps of branches, then troweling it all deep down.

She stroked the good earth with the rake.

Tiller in hand she readied rows for wildflower seeds.

WANT TO PUKE!

For the first time in her life Yolande felt like what she was.

An only child.

A terrified one, as she didn't know how to be alone.

Along with Saturdays, she was starting to hate Sundays, when after church Savannah said she couldn't go for a bite to eat because of schoolwork to finish up. Why?

Because she spent Saturdays at that stupid school.

Sundays were becoming unbearable too because on their way to and from church Savannah went on and on about a place that might as well have been the moon.

Savannah was going to learn to play basketball. "Promise, Yolande, you won't tell Mother."

Mona was teaching her Creole.

The girls from Liberia had supposedly made the most delicious dish. Some kind of stupid stew with something called froofroo or foofoo. Too close to voodoo for Yolande.

"And next week, from Cassandra—she's from Jamaica— I'll learn how to make pepper pot soup."

The thought of *that* made Yolande want to puke!

Fridays were vexing too because Savannah was so looking forward to a Saturday without her.

Each time Savannah urged, "You really should come one Saturday!" Yolande's stomach burned.

RISE UP! RISE UP! RISE UP!

Hours after sowing wildflower seeds, Savannah was all cleaned up, every bit of dirt beneath her fingernails gone. She was out of work clothes and back into her dusty-rose shirt-waist. She had a big matching bow at her nape, tied around her braid.

And she was grateful.

Grateful that her parents had said she could stay into the evening, attend Nannie Burroughs's lecture.

Of course there was a condition.

"You must wait for me in the main house or outside Pioneer Hall, not down the hill," said Father.

Entering Alpha Hall's auditorium, tan coat over one arm, Savannah spotted several girls she knew, speculated that the older women and men in the crowd were Lincoln Heights townsfolk. She was about to head for Elza and Rosetta when she spotted Nella. She beamed. She hadn't seen her since Miss Gertie was back right as rain.

Savannah hurried over. "How good to see you, Nella!"

Nella seemed a little taken aback when Savannah hugged her, then sat in one of the empty seats on either side.

"Have you heard that I've been helping out here on Saturdays?"

"Yes, I have. And I've heard nothing but good things about you."

"This seat taken?" said the wearer of brown cap toe shoes.

Savannah looked up to see Lloyd in a fairly nice brown sack suit over a blue-and-white-striped club collar percale shirt and a brown skinny knit tie. He had a felt Knox hat in his hand.

"By all means," said Savannah, facing front.

The hubbub ceased when Mona stepped out onto the stage. Introduction done, applause begun, Nannie Burroughs emerged from behind the curtain in a black serge suit.

She paced a bit, hands behind her back, before stepping up to the podium. She said nothing until the applause died down.

"I was asked by a southern white woman," began Nannie Burroughs, "a southern white woman who is an enthusiastic worker for votes for white women, 'What can the Negro woman do with the ballot?'"

A smattering of laughter.

Nannie Burroughs cocked her head to the side. "Said I to that woman, 'What can she do *without* it?'"

"Tell it! Tell it!"

"When the ballot is put into the hands of the American

woman the world is going to get a correct estimate of the Negro woman."

The audience erupted into cheers, applause.

Tone, rhythm, musicality. This wasn't a lecture. This was preaching, Baptist preaching.

"When the ballot is put into the hand of the American woman it will find the Negro woman a tower of strength of which poets have never sung—"

"Speak on!"

"Of which orators have never spoken—"

"Amen! Amen! Amen!"

"Of which scholars have never written!"

Savannah was on the edge of her seat. *If only I had a mother like Nannie Burroughs, so bold, so strong, fierce.*

Savannah sat spellbound by the passion, the power as Nannie Burroughs rolled on, singing the praises of Harriet Tubman, Sojourner Truth, Maria W. Stewart, the Forten women, Mary Ann Shadd Cary, Biddy Mason, Clara Brown.

"How is it that Elizabeth Keckley rose up out of slavery to become one of the most sought-after modistes in white society—right here in the capital?"

Applause.

"How is it that Maggie Lena Walker born, as she is so very, very fond of saying, 'not with a silver spoon in my mouth but a laundry basket practically on my head'—how is it that she rose up to found one of the most successful Negro banks in this land?"

More applause.

"How is it that Sissieretta Jones, the daughter of folks born in slavery—how is it that she rose up to become a world-class concert singer, charming the ears of royalty?"

Applause.

"How is it—"

Nannie Burroughs paused, shook a clenched fist in the air.

"Imagine how much more Negro women can achieve when women have the national vote, the right, as the honorable Frederick Douglass used to say, 'by which all others are secured.'"

Looking wise, steadfast, ready to head a parade, Principal Burroughs pointed out into the audience.

"My sisters, I say to you, rise up, rise up, rise up! Rise up for woman suffrage. Get up petitions! Flood Congress with letters. Bombard that Woodrow Wilson with letters. Negro men, I say to you, don't hinder your womenfolk—your mothers, your wives, your sisters, your daughters. Stand not in front of them. Stand alongside them!"

The crowd was on its feet. The applause would have shaken a weaker building's rafters.

ALL DAY?

Yolande was returning from a Lillian Evans concert with her parents when she saw Mr. Riddle tinkering with his car.

"What's the trouble, Wyatt?" her father asked.

"Won't start."

"Didn't you have a fella here working on it recently?"

"Indeed. And what's that about a fool and his money?" Mr. Riddle laughed. "Won't be using him again."

Yolande looked up at the Riddle living room window to see if Savannah was looking out.

With the hood of his car still up, Mr. Riddle asked, "Oscar, do me a favor, see if it'll crank now."

Yolande's father got behind the wheel. The car started.

"Keep it going while I pop back in and wash my hands." Mr. Riddle closed the hood.

"Is Savannah in, Mr. Riddle?"

"No. I'm on my way to pick her up. She begged us to let her attend a lecture at Nannie Burroughs's school."

"She's been there all day?"

FAR-OFF HOPES AND DREAMS

It was more than a minute before the clapping ceased, before Nannie Burroughs left the podium, stepped behind the curtain, before people filed out dropping coins into baskets the Allen twins held on either side of the door, before Savannah, Nella, and Lloyd made their way out of Alpha Hall and over to Pioneer's porch.

"We'll wait with you until your father arrives," Nella had said.

Savannah was beaming. "Nannie Burroughs is a tonic!"

"That she is," replied Nella.

"She's a strong, strong woman," said Lloyd, "but too bad she don't see the big picture. Why she thinking woman suffrage will change anything?"

Savannah was flabbergasted. "You don't support woman suffrage?"

"I'm not against it. I just don't think it will make a difference for Negroes."

"When women have the national vote, we will be able to vote in just people."

"How many white women you think will vote for people who want justice for Negro people? Wunna never read about how white women turn out for lynchings with picnic baskets and they children?"

"But—"

"The bulk of Negro people live in the South, right?"

"Yes," replied Savannah.

"And how long Negro men have national suffrage?"

Savannah did the math in her head. "Going on fifty years."

"And going on fifty years, don't the white men in the South do everything in their power, terrorizing people, to keep as many Negro men as possible from voting?"

Yes, there were poll taxes, literacy tests. Savannah had also heard of Negro men beaten, murdered even for trying to vote, of black families kicked off land they leased because the Mister talked of casting a ballot. "But—"

"Now how many white women *ever* stand up for the Negro man to keep his right to vote?"

One, two, a couple of names came to mind, but not enough to counter Lloyd.

Savannah felt small and at a loss too. Why was Nannie Burroughs—like other women in the Association—so on fire for the Anthony amendment to pass? Was there really no point in the "Votes for Women" flyers Mother had her design, flyers handed out in churches, at the Negro Ys, during steamboat outings, picnics?

Months back Savannah had asked her parents why they

were so keen on the Anthony amendment, seeing as how people in the District couldn't vote for president, had no senators, no representatives.

"We live not for ourselves alone," Father had replied.

"Some things we crusade for are urgent," said Mother. "Take lynching. That abomination needs to stop immediately! Other things we crusade for are in service of our far-off hopes and dreams."

Savannah turned to Lloyd. "We have far-off hopes and dreams, you know!"

Lloyd snickered. "Far-off hopes . . . See, the problem with wunna is that wunna want to work within the system—my kind say the system needs overturning, just like the earth in spring so we reap good things. Wunna say, oh, if we get a good education, if we speak like the white man, if we don't laugh out loud or wear red, if we vote . . ."

"What are you talking about? What system?"

Under Lloyd's piercing gaze Savannah felt a bit of a nitwit.

"The capitalist system."

Nella's mouth was poked out. "Let us speak of something else."

"Let me guess," sneered Lloyd. "Your parents belong to societies dedicated to uplifting the race, right?"

"Well, yes."

"And they subscribe to magazines like the *Crisis*."

"Well, yes."

"And I *bet* they didn't even say a peep when that Du Bois fella betrayed the race."

"Dr. Du Bois never betrayed us!" Savannah was livid.

"Close Ranks." Lloyd practically spat.

"Close what?"

"When America entered the war, he urged Negroes to rally round the flag, to 'forget our special grievances' while the war is raging 'and close our ranks shoulder to shoulder with our own white fellow citizens.'" Lloyd paused. "So Negroes closed ranks, rallied round the flag. Negro men went off to war and—"

Nella tapped Lloyd on the shoulder. "Please, let's just enjoy this wonderful evening air. Stop! Stop your friction!"

Lloyd turned to Nella. "Lemme finish, lemme open she eyes, save she from delusion."

Rosetta popped out of Pioneer Hall. "Savannah, your father just called. He had trouble with the car but hopes to be here soon."

"Thank you," said Savannah.

And Lloyd went back to having his say. "So Negroes close ranks. Did lynching stop? Can you or I eat in any restaurant we please in this town? Thousands of Negro men fought like tigers in the so-called war to make the world safe for democracy, and what have they gotten for their trouble?"

"New York City gave the 369th a grand parade."

Lloyd laughed. "Can a parade fill bellies? Can a parade raise wages?" His fury, like the moon, was rising. "That 'Closed Ranks' editorial of Du Bois was as stupid as his notion that the salvation of the race will be folks like *you*. You so-called Talented Tenth. Hogwash!"

"Hogwash?"

No one puts down Dr. Du Bois!

"Dr. Du Bois probably never sleeps. He spends all his time fighting for the race!" Savannah paused to compose herself. "And you're wrong about the Talented Tenth." For the first time in a long time Savannah was proud of her parents. "My father's insurance company employs over twenty people. He has agents in Baltimore and in other places. He provides insurance for Negroes whitefolks won't do business with. Father gives generously to the NAACP, to our church, and to, to—have you heard of Camp Pleasant?"

Lloyd shook his head.

"It's for the less fortunate women and children. Father gives money to that too!"

Nella paced the porch. "All this politics is getting on my nerves."

And Savannah stood taller.

"My mother is a member of the National Association of Colored Women. They saved Frederick Douglass's estate. They are always raising money to help the poor. At Thanksgiving, at Christmas, at Easter, they—"

"Lemme guess, they make up baskets of food, pack up clothes they tired of."

"There's nothing to be said for feeding and clothing people?"

"People need more than patches."

Savannah glared at Lloyd. "Well, what's your solution?"

Lloyd glared back. "Workers of the world unite!"

Savannah couldn't keep her eyes from going wide. "You're a—a socialist?" she whispered.

"I'm not a party member. But I see eye to eye with a lot of the thinking. Your kind favor reform. My kind revolution."

The black Buick pulled up.

Lloyd whipped out something from his pocket, shoved it into Savannah's hand.

"What's this?"

"Things you need to ponder."

In the darkness Savannah couldn't make out all of the magazine's title. Just the *Mess*—. She tucked the magazine into the pocket of her coat, headed down the steps. Nella, Lloyd followed.

"Hello, Nella!" said Father when the three reached the car.

"Evening, Mr. Riddle, sir."

"Father, this is Nella's cousin Lloyd."

"Pleased to meet you."

"Likewise."

"Can we give you a lift?" asked Savannah.

"Oh, no, Miss Riddle, that's not necessary." But Nella sounded awfully half-hearted.

"Oh, hop in, you two," said Father.

Lloyd looked away. "We can take the—"

Nella elbowed Lloyd.

Savannah tried not to laugh.

"If you're sure it won't put you out, Mr. Riddle, sir," said Nella.

Savannah moved to sit up front, then stopped. "Lloyd,

you sit next to Father so Nella and I can sit together in the back."

Unable to get but a peep out of Nella about her day, about *anything*, Savannah tuned in to the talk up front.

Lloyd worked some days as a mechanic at the Belt railway company, she learned as she listened to him tell Father the likely root cause of his car trouble. Lloyd also did construction work on the hotel John Lewis was putting up on 13th and T.

"Some sight that will be!" said Father. "The District's first high-class hotel for our people."

Lloyd shook his head. "I gotta say that I find it curious he choose to name it the Whitelaw."

Father humphed. "Never thought of it that way. But you see, Whitelaw is his mother's maiden name." After a pause Father asked, "Think it will open on schedule?"

"If things keep going as planned," replied Lloyd.

Hypocrite! thought Savannah. *He runs down the Talented Tenth but works for a man like John Lewis, who owns the Industrial Savings Bank! Can't get more capitalist than that!*

When Father turned onto Nella and Lloyd's street, Savannah observed that it was a bit nicer than the street of drab row houses, Barrows' Meat Market, and the Open Eye Saloon, the street that had sent her into a panic weeks back. The row house he parked in front of was a simple, sturdy brick number. The staircase's latticed risers were in something like a fleur-de-lis pattern. The building had an arched lintel above recessed double doors, and there were lovely cream crocheted curtains at the three-quarter-length windowpanes of those double doors. In a downstairs window was a neat sign: BOARD AND ROOMS.

"How fortuitous," Nella said. "I just remembered that your kind mother's order is in. If you give me a minute—"

"Let me come up with you and get it," Savannah offered.

"Oh, no," said Nella, emerging from the car.

"It'll spare you a trip back down." Savannah got out of the car. "I'm sure you're knocked off your feet," she added, caring nothing about Nella's feet but curious to see how they lived.

What did that make her? Savannah wondered as she and Nella headed up the stairs, leaving Lloyd and Father before the hood of the car.

HELLO, MISS FINE LADY

The third-floor apartment was tiny.

Its kitchen couldn't hold but two people at a time, maybe three if skinny.

The inscrutable Miss Gertie rose from an old broad-back mahogany-and-cane armchair, a crochet hook and yarn in her hands.

"Good evening, Miss Riddle."

"Good evening, Miss Gertie," said Savannah. "And please, Miss Gertie, don't stand on my account."

"Mr. Riddle was good enough to give us a ride home," said Nella. "Savannah come up to get Mrs. Riddle's product." Nella turned to Savannah with a smile. "I won't be but a jiffy."

Savannah's eyes followed Nella, saw a door on the right, another, narrower, at the end of the hall. A bedroom, a bathroom she guessed.

She figured Lloyd slept in the front room, on the metal cot with a chenille bedspread near the small window. Someone, she guessed Lloyd, had concocted a way to hang a curtain from the ceiling that could be drawn around the cot.

Miss Gertie sure loved to crochet.

There was a stack of crocheted doilies on the table by her chair.

Crocheted doilies on the chair and on the small settee.

Crocheted runner on the small round table in the center of the room. On it, cut-glass salt and paper shakers and violets in a wide-mouth mason jar.

Around the table were two matching oak fiddleback chairs and a lath-back chair of a different wood.

The place was neat as a pin. Savannah caught a whiff of Lysol F&F.

"Here you are," said Nella. She handed Savannah a mint-green crocheted bag. "Do tell her I thank her kindly for the order and I hope she will continue to use Poro products."

"Hello, Miss Fine Lady!" Bim shot up from the bottom step as Savannah exited the building.

"Hello there, Bim." Savannah reached into her purse, brought out a dime.

The hood was up. Father stood before it watching Lloyd work a wrench.

"It won't start?" asked Savannah.

"It will," replied Lloyd. "Just making some adjustments so it will still start ten years from now."

Work done, hood down, Father and Lloyd wiped their hands on rags, then shook.

Savannah moved to open the door to the front seat—

Lloyd beat her to it.

"Why, thank you, Lloyd."

As the car pulled off Savannah looked back. She was touched by the way Lloyd took Bim by the hand, led him down the street.

MONKEY-CHASING, TREE-CLIMBING . . .

How about Gaskins'?" asked Yolande.

No.

Dade's?

No.

Board's? Lee's Lunch Room? The—?

No.

No.

No.

"Well, after we change our clothes let's go for a walk."

"I had a long day yesterday. I just want to stay in."

They were yards behind their parents, en route from church.

Yolande stopped. Arms at her sides. Fists balled up.

Savannah stopped too. "Yolande, look—"

"No, *you* look, Savannah! *Weeks* ago you apologized for being so beastly to me. But ever since you've taken up with that monkey-chasing, tree-climbing Nella and started spending Saturdays at that stupid school, you've been downright—"

"What did you call Nella?"

"You heard me."

"Who is being beastly—downright ugly now, Yolande? How could you say such things? West Indians, Africans . . . they are, well, like our cousins. We are all Negro, Yolande. More alike than not."

Yolande's fury, her fear made her deaf, blind to all reason.

"You've been eating strange food out there. It's like that Nella has put a spell on you."

"Nella isn't even there on Saturdays! But you know what? If she was I'd be past glad."

"But what about me!" Yolande stamped her foot.

"What about you, Yolande? How many times have I asked you to come with me? But, no, you want to stay in your—your little cocoon."

They were walking again, picking up their pace.

Yolande felt a crushing shame over her outburst. *I've gone and done it now!*

A few steps later Savannah gave her hope.

"Tell you what. After you change, come over."

Yolande vowed to contain herself. To not say another harsh word about Nella or Nannie Burroughs's school.

THREE CRUDE WOODEN STEPS

First, as workers, black and white, we all have one common interest . . ."

Higher wages.

Shorter work days.

Good working conditions.

None of that struck Savannah as unreasonable, nor wholly impossible.

She had read A. Philip Randolph's editorial the night before. On that Sunday afternoon, while waiting for Yolande—wondering what on earth they'd talk about, do, wondering if she'd run out of patience with her again—Savannah decided to reread Randolph's piece, "Our Reason for Being."

"The introduction of women and children into the factories proves that capitalists are only concerned with profits and that they will exploit any race or class—"

The footsteps had to be hers. Sure enough, within seconds a contrite-looking Yolande poked her head in, then bounced into the room. Something behind her back.

Savannah put the magazine down.

"Sorry for the things I said earlier." Yolande was almost at Savannah's bed, eyes down and fidgety. "Here." She handed Savannah a peach ribbon necklette. "You look better in this color than I do."

"Why, thank—"

Yolande shrieked.

"What is it?"

Yolande grabbed the magazine, waved it in the air. "You're reading the *Messenger*? You must throw it in the trash! No, tear it up into a million tiny pieces! *Burn* it!"

Savannah snatched the magazine back. "What's wrong with you?"

"It's a—" Yolande lowered her voice. "It's a *socialist* magazine."

"Yes. So?" Last night Savannah had hidden the magazine between her mattress and box springs. But she wasn't about to admit that to Yolande.

"Father says the men who put it out are also *atheists*!"

"Yes, Yolande, they are socialists and . . ."

Savannah didn't know what to do with "atheists." She didn't know anyone who wasn't Baptist or Methodist, who flat-out just didn't believe in God.

I'm not a party member. But I see eye to eye with a lot of the thinking. That's what Lloyd had said. *Was he an atheist too?*

"And socialists are like anarchists, like Reds, Savannah!" Yolande was hysterical, pale cheeks flaming red.

"I've never heard of socialists planting bombs or calling for the obliteration of government. Seems to me they simply

want people—well, like factory workers, builders, mechanics—
to have better lives all around."

"You're wrong! Father says that people like that Eugene
Debs, they want people like us to give up *everything* we have.
They want common people to run things. And Debs looks a
lot like that devil Lenin who's behind all that Bolshevik Red
Terror in Russia. They're killing rich people right and left."

"The *Messenger* isn't calling for anyone to be—"

"I'm telling you, Savannah, getting caught with a magazine like that could—"

"What?"

"Land you in big, big, a heap of trouble."

"Yolande, I don't need you to—"

"I'm trying to *save* you, Savannah!"

"From what?"

"From yourself!"

"I don't need saving!"

"Girls . . . Everything all right in there?"

Mother on the landing.

"We're fine," replied Savannah. "Just having a lively debate."

After Yolande practically fled the room, Savannah returned
to the *Messenger*. Between one page and the next, she found a
newspaper clipping.

"The New Politics for the New Negro" by Hubert H.
Harrison.

Magnetic. Commanding. Insistent. A subtle poetry in the

prose as he wrote of something called Swadesha, something called Sinn Fein, of the Negro plight.

One line stood out. "The world, as it ought to be, is still for us, as for others, the world that does not exist."

As for others? Who are these others?

When Savannah was next out at Lincoln Heights, this time assigned to the store, Lloyd was nowhere to be found.

She left an envelope for Nella. Inside, a note:

Dear Nella,
Please return this magazine to Lloyd and tell him that I thank him for it.

The time after that, Mona handed Savannah a thick package. "Nella left this for you."

Inside the package a note:

Dear Savannah:
I thought you might find this interesting.
This book is about thirty years old but millions
of people in the land of the free still live like this.
Thousands in this city. Negroes in the shadow of
the Capitol.

Note tucked into the book, Savannah scanned the title. The red lettering made her think of a Charles Dickens tale.

Above the title a sketch of three barefoot boys huddled together, shivering maybe.

Beneath the title a warren of bleak, haunted-looking tenements.

Later that night, in an eyelet-trimmed ice-blue nightgown and tucked between crisp, clean sheets, Savannah went randomly through the book's drawings.

"In the home of an Italian rag-picker, Jersey street," read one caption.

Home? More like a closet or stall.

Rough walls, wooden bucket, tin tubs, bundles stuffed, Savannah assumed, with rags. And the woman cradling a baby, she was looking up. In anger? Fear? Despair?

"Lodgers in a Crowded Bayard Street Tenement—'Five cents a spot.'"

Grimy men on pallets. Clothes hanging haphazard on nails in walls. A pair of beat-up boots before a filthy little stove.

Her home was a palace in comparison.

Whole families living in a single room; some looked to be about half the size of their parlor, Charlie's old room, Mother's sewing room that doubled as another guest room.

Savannah paged back to the introduction: "Long ago it was said that 'one half of the world does not know how the other half lives.' That was true then. It did not know because it did not care."

Savannah studied more illustrations.

"Upstairs in Blindman's Alley."

"Bandits' Roost."

"Bottle Alley."

And these were mostly whitefolks.

Dear Lloyd,

Thank you for the book. I want to see how the other half lives here. Our people. You said in the shadow of the Capitol.

There was no note needed as it turned out on that April day. Lloyd was whitewashing outbuildings. He was just about done with one near the largest garden plot, ground already sown with early crops. Cucumbers. Lettuces. Spinach. Pole beans.

"So you feeling yuhself brave enough?" He was playful, not mean.

Savannah nodded her head. "Plenty brave!"

Lloyd paused, whitewash brush in mid-air. "Can you get away Tuesday afternoon?"

Savannah thought fast. "Yes, I can manage that." Tuesday was cold dinner day because Mother spent the afternoon and early evening at Cedar Hill. "Say four o'clock?"

Lloyd nodded. "We meet on the edge of the Capitol lawn?"

Savannah nodded, then dashed off to the library with a

satchel of books she was donating. After that she headed to Pioneer Hall to assist Mona with paperwork.

It seemed a forever walk, deeper, deeper into Southwest. On they walked until they came to a place Savannah found more frightening than that street of drab row houses, Barrows' Meat Market, and the Open Eye Saloon.

Alley after alley, crammed-together shanties.

Crude wood.

Crumbling brick.

Tar paper roofs.

"They call this area Beggars' Bay," said Lloyd. He had stopped at the mouth of an alley. Entering, he reached back for Savannah's hand.

Savannah was glad for that hand, rough but warm and pulsing good, as she sidestepped broken glass, rusted tin cans, spied pot-bellied barefoot boys, girls. A shriveled old woman in a battered bonnet, filthy striped skirt, and plaid blouse staggered past.

Grown-ups cussed, babies wailed.

Savannah smelled grease, gases, greens, human waste.

A rat skittered across their path.

How many newspapers report scenes like this?

A one-eyed mangy cat gave chase.

And this?

Savannah tightened her grip on Lloyd's hand.

"No indoor plumbing," he whispered.

Newspapers to windows.

On page one, or two—anywhere in the paper?

Pipes, busted buckets, table legs, rags, fence planks, strewn upon the ground.

Mother's sermons on how blessed she and Charlie were . . .

Random stories about people to whom the Association gave food, clothes . . .

Passing by, in the street, grinders, cart men, washerwomen, chimney sweeps, tinkers . . .

The sight of veterans missing arms, legs . . .

Illustrations of Bandits' Roost, Bottle Alley . . .

None of it compared to standing amid such dense and pressing need.

Her emerald velvet-and-chiffon dress . . . her silver dancing shoes, the white evening gloves, that silver-and-rhinestone peacock-shaped hairpin . . . It could probably feed a family for a week—or more, maybe a whole month! Now that would be some *real* renewal.

"No electricity," Lloyd whispered, giving Savannah's hand a squeeze.

One home had an old headboard as a door. Faded lettering on the brick revealed the dwelling's history as a stable.

A little boy, watchful, wary, hunched atop a mound of rubble, was wolfing down a piece of bread with one hand, clutching a well-worn book in the other.

The forgettable, the forgotten.

"Lloyd!"

A husky man with a bent back lumbered down into the alley.

"Brother Spencer!"

The two men embraced.

"You coming to the meeting on Thursday night, right?"

"Be there!"

"Bring everybody who work with you at the Navy Yard."

"Lined up already!"

"Good man!" said Lloyd. "I'll see you then."

Seconds after the bent-back man headed farther down the alley, Lloyd checked his pocket watch. "Enough for one day?"

Savannah nodded. "What happened to him, his back? Spencer, is it?"

"He fell off a scaffold at the Yard. He didn't stay bandaged up and in bed long enough."

"Why on earth not?"

"Mouths to feed."

"He lives here?"

Lloyd shook his head. "But he got family here."

They were near a home outside of which a middle-aged woman in a housedress and boots was working a water pump. Nearby a girl in a faded red-check pinafore dress, with a proud, alert bearing, was sweeping three crude wooden steps.

This needs to be on the front of every *newspaper,* every day!

"You are right, Lloyd," Savannah whispered, heartsick

and roiling with rage. They were back again at the mouth of the alley. "People need more than patches. They need . . ."

Steps away and they were still holding hands.

"It's so much," said Savannah. "It's so big." She multiplied that alley by ten, twenty. And that was just in the District.

"We need a big change," said Lloyd. "Big change in how we all see, how we all think."

"'The world, as it ought to be,'" Savannah whispered.

They passed small churches, saloons, pawnshops, dilapidated wood-frame buildings, barrels and bushel baskets, a barbershop with its prices stenciled in the window. Shave ten cents. Haircut twenty-five. In the cellar below a cobbler's shop.

A streetcar clanged by.

Savannah found an excuse to retrieve a handkerchief from her handbag—self-conscious, unnerved by how long she and Lloyd had walked hand in hand.

"You're more brave than I thought, Miss Ting," he said. "You held up good."

Back at the edge of the Capitol lawn, Lloyd tipped his hat, tapped the top of Savannah's nose. "Smile, Miss Ting. When you get too down about people's plight, then you're in no shape to act."

Savannah managed a half smile, held it, wishing her hand again in his.

Lloyd was just a few feet on his way back deeper into Southwest when Savannah called out, "Lloyd?"

He spun around, returned. "Yeah?"

"That meeting you mentioned to Spencer, what is that about?"

"I give talks about how capitalism works, how the big-big wealth grows on the backs of we little people, how the system need to change."

PATHETIC!

Yolande flew from her house when Savannah turned onto the block.

She was on the bottom step when Savannah reached her walkway.

"I saw you!"

"Saw me what?" Savannah's eyes narrowed.

"I saw you leave your house looking like you were about to work in the garden! I followed you. I saw you meet that common-looking man too black for comfort."

Yolande took a step back. Savannah was spitting mad, and for a moment Yolande feared Savannah might even slap her.

"Have you forgotten that my father is dark-skinned?"

"But he's not blue black. And he's a credit to the race."

Savannah rolled her eyes. "How do you know that this 'common-looking' man, as you put it—his name is Lloyd, by the way, and he's Nella's cousin—how do you know he's not a credit to the race? Huh? Tell me that, Miss Know-It-All! Or perhaps I should make that Miss Know-*Nothing*!"

Yolande swallowed. "Well, I'm going to tell your parents!"

"Go ahead. Tell them! After what I've seen today . . ."

"What?"

Savannah turned away. "Nothing that you would care about." She took a few more steps, then made an about-face.

Yolande jittered inside beneath Savannah's steely glare.

"You know what, Yolande . . . I don't want to walk with you to school, from school. I don't want you to talk to me *at* school." Her voice was low but hard. "I don't want to go with you to Board's or anywhere else *ever* again!"

"But—"

"I can't take you anymore, Yolande! You're a worm, ridiculous, *pathetic*! And if you also want to tell my parents what I just said, fine!"

As Savannah hurried into her house, tears flooded Yolande's face.

Why did I follow her? Why did I say those awful things? Why can't I stop myself from making her angry? Yolande beat her fists against her temples, slid down the fence, still sobbing.

Surely the friendship was now blown to smithereens.

A few days later, real bombs were in the news—a bomb plot that shook the world as Yolande knew it.

MORE CHAOS TO COME

"U.S. HUNTS ANARCHISTS AS MAY DAY MAIL PLOT FAILS TO GAIN VICTIMS."

More than thirty bombs.

Packages the size of biscuit tins.

Dressed up as samples from Gimbel Brothers in New York City.

Thanks to insufficient postage, about half never reached their destinations.

Targeted: Seattle mayor Ola Hanson, proud of his iron-fist approach toward striking workers.

Targeted: Former Georgia Senator Thomas W. Hardwick, proud cosponsor of a bill that gave the government free rein to deport immigrants who were anarchists, even immigrants caught with anarchist propaganda.

Targeted: Other champions of kicking immigrants out of the country, especially Italians, Germans, Russians.

Targeted: capitalists John D. Rockefeller, J. P. Morgan.

Targeted: Supreme Court Justice Oliver Wendell Holmes Jr. He had penned the High Court's unanimous ruling upholding a lower court's decision to sentence Eugene Debs to ten years' imprisonment and to strip him of his citizenship.

Postmasters everywhere were on high alert and Savannah seized by a sense of more chaos to come.

She turned to page two of the *Star* for more on the bomb plot. Immediately her eyes fastened upon a diagram.

Percussion caps.

Metal burrs.

Bottle filled with acid.

Dynamite.

She felt out of body, out of time as her eyes glided down to a big ad for Leverton's on G Street, boasting "THE LARGEST BLOUSE DEPARTMENT IN THE CITY."

Who could care about new blouses at such a time as this?

Savannah put down the *Star*.

By sundown Father had gotten word to his employees that the office would be closed the next day. He later brought up from the basement a metal chest, and from the garden shed, a stake and a toolbox. "Pumpkin, bring me a sheet from one of your large sketch pads and a marking pen."

When a still-numb Savannah joined Father in the front yard with its petunias, begonias, its dogwood tree, she began to tremble as she watched him put the metal box on a patch of lawn right behind the gate, pound the stake into the ground.

Then he took the sheet of paper, the pen, stooped down on the ground with both, wrote:

*Mr. Parker, please deposit
all mail in this box.*

Father nailed the sign to the stake.

"Just a precaution," he said, closing up that toolbox. "I don't think we have anything to worry about. Just a precaution."

"*Please*, Lloyd, be careful," Savannah whispered to the night. She was standing on her balcony trying to be calm, trying not to cry.

The authorities wouldn't just round up anarchists. They'd hunt down Reds, socialists, *anybody* branded radical.

I give talks about how capitalism works, how the big-big wealth grows on the backs of we little people, how the system need to change.

"*Please*, Lloyd, be careful."

TWO WEAK WHIMPERS

Like a peregrine clutching prey in its claws, fear had a tight grip on the capital.

People jumped, scattered when a car backfired.

Streets eerie like at the height of Spanish flu.

Talking less.

Whispering more.

No strolling. Hurried gaits.

Eyes straight ahead or cast on the ground.

Savannah was returning from school on the Monday after May Day when two Model Ts whipped around the corner. They screeched to a halt before the Pinchbacks' Tudor-like townhouse.

Out poured one, two, three, four, five burly white men.

Black suits.

Black fedoras.

They barreled to the door.

"Open up!" one boomed as he banged.

Another began banging. "Open up!"

Quick as she could, Savannah made it to her house,

saw Mother in the living room window, saw Yolande and her mother in theirs.

"Mother! Mother! What's going on?"

By the time Savannah joined Mother at the window, the Pinchbacks' front door was kicked in, the last of the white men surging forward.

Bumping. Banging. Thudding. Slaps. Punches.

Angry, growling commands.

Things crashed, shattered.

Shouts.

Mrs. Pinchback's screams.

Between a tick and a tock two men dragged pudgy Mr. Pinchback from the house. His collarless white shirt, suspenders, trousers splattered with blood that ran down the side of his face, from his nose. Without his glasses, he was a stumbler in the night.

Two more men hauled out a squirming Mrs. Pinchback, her housedress ripped in places. She bit. She kicked.

They slapped.

Little Sebastian scampered out growling, yapped, snapped, nipped at ankles.

The fifth man emerged from the house, drew his revolver.

Savannah looked away, buried her head in Mother's bosom, heard—

Bang!

Then two weak whimpers.

FROZEN

He was a haberdasher: Pinchback's Toggery Shop on Seventh near T Street.

Father purchased much of his clothing there.

Savannah passed it whenever she went to Uncle Madison's or to just have a walk about U Street.

Mrs. Pinchback gave music lessons in their home—had been her and Yolande's piano teacher.

Savannah joined Mother in tears.

"Why did they do this? What could the Pinchbacks have—?"

Mother settled her on the davenport. "I must telephone your father."

Savannah was in the vestibule when he turned into the walkway. She flung the door open, ran out, sobbed anew. "It was horrible! Absolutely horrible! Blood all over him!"

Father had made the fifteen-minute walk in ten.

No sooner than they were inside, the telephone rang.

"I'll get it." In a few fast strides Father was beside the hallway table where the telephone sat.

Savannah and Mother huddled by his side.

He lifted the receiver from the switch hook. "Riddle residence . . . Hello, Calvin . . . They're fine . . . Good Lord!"

Father winced.

"What time was this? . . . Uh-huh . . . I agree . . . Who else? . . . Here is good."

He looked at Mother, raised his left hand with fingers splayed.

"Savannah, dear, please help me prepare some light refreshments?"

"Right," Savannah heard Father say before he hung up.

Savannah laid squares of cheese on soda crackers, sliced bread, spread potted meat. All with trembling hands and so glad for something to do.

Father entered the kitchen, headed for the back door.

"Where are you going?" Savannah practically shrieked, on pause from placing her makings on a tray.

Mother covered a pot of eggs with water, placed the pot on the stove, turned on the burner.

"Oscar and I will bury the dog and board up the front door."

"Is that safe? What if more white men come—"

"Lightning never strikes the same place twice, pumpkin."

"They will be all right," said Mother with Father long gone. "They will be all right."

It sounded less an assurance, more a prayer.

Mother was putting on a brave face, Savannah knew. Her voice too calm, her movements stiff, not fluid. And she had seen Mother's hands shaking when putting those eggs into a white enamelware pot.

Now Mother was cutting up celery and carrots. "Bring me two celery trays and a large relish dish. The sawtooth ones, please."

And Mother seemed hard-pressed to look her in the eye. Was she trying to shield her from the fright in her own? Was she afraid of questions that might arise?

First came Calvin Chase and John Lewis. Then Hannibal Bash and Waylon Jones, finally Yolande's father.

Savannah took jackets and hats, ushered them into the living room, where Mother had laid out food and drink.

After the small talk died down Father slid the living room doors closed.

"Come," said Mother, removing her apron and signaling Savannah to remove hers. "We are going next door."

Yolande was still in her living room bay window.

Frozen.

SAME SPOON-BACK CHAISE

Girls, why don't you go up to Yolande's room," urged Mrs. Holloway, leading Yolande from their living room.

She looked, moved like a zombie.

Once the girls were up in her room, Yolande threw herself onto her bed, curled up into a ball.

As Savannah moved near—

"Close the door!"

Savannah was on the edge of Yolande's bed a good five minutes before Yolande said a word.

"I overheard Mother on the telephone. Mrs. Lee, I think. Then she called Mrs. Sanderson."

"About the Pinchbacks?"

Yolande nodded, burst into tears. "Communists," she whispered.

Savannah frowned. "But—" The Pinchbacks were quiet, orderly, upstanding. "Are you sure?"

Yolande nodded again. "Only recently though." Yolande

wiped her eyes, began to rock. "Remember that nephew they lost in the war?"

"Yeah."

"Not killed in battle like we were told. A white officer shot him in the back because he refused to answer to . . . an ugly word . . . The Pinchbacks couldn't forgive the army, America for that."

Yolande's face was contorted; she was practically writhing in pain. "What if . . ."

"What if what?"

"What if we had been in their house for a piano lesson when those men came?"

"It's been years since we had piano lessons."

"Well, what if, like that time Mrs. Pinchback was sick and—and—Mother had us take over a casserole. What if we had been there, Savannah!"

Savannah rubbed Yolande's shoulder. "But we weren't there."

"What if the government finds out she was our piano teacher?—that we spent time in their home!"

Seeing Yolande in such a state, Savannah became increasingly worried about her friend. More so when Yolande faced the wall, thrust a thumb into her mouth.

I thought she had given that up years ago.

Yolande's near-paralyzing fright reeled Savannah back to the raid.

Bloodied Mr. Pinchback.

His manhandled wife.

Bang!

"You *can't* let it take you, Yolande! You *can't* let it take you! The world isn't coming to an end! Think instead about what you, what I, what we can do to make it better."

As Savannah struggled to come up with some gesture, some better words of comfort, it dawned on her that it had been a very long time since she had been in Yolande's bedroom.

Same ivory bedroom suite as hers—chiffonier, dresser, cane panel bed, wardrobe, dressing table with triptych mirror.

Same Cinderella desk and matching desk chair.

Same spoon-back chaise.

Only difference in their rooms was that, instead of yellow, Yolande's mother had opted for pink when it came to wallpaper and upholstery.

And the dollhouse.

Savannah rose, stepped over to the far wall. "I can't believe you still have this."

"What's wrong with that?" whimpered Yolande.

"Nothing. Nothing's wrong with it at all." Savannah really wasn't being judgmental. She was truly shocked.

She had gotten rid of her dollhouse years ago, had packed it up and taken it down to Mother's giveaway corner of the basement.

And not only did Yolande still have hers . . .

Savannah remembered shifting things around in her dollhouse—moving the dining room's tiny vase of flowers from the sideboard to the table, rearranging tables, chairs, the sofa in the parlor.

Yolande's dollhouse was exactly as it had always been.

Pink silk divan still against the back wall.

Still before the window, the jardiniere overflowing with moss and pink roses.

Chairs, tables—everything—exactly where Yolande had placed them all those years ago. Peering closer still, Savannah saw that everything—every stick of furniture, every ornament, every tiny piece of china—was spotless. Not a speck of dust. Mirrors above mantels gleamed.

A twinge of guilt, a pang, a stab.

How harsh, cruel she had been.

You're a worm, ridiculous, pathetic*!*

Yes, Yolande was shallow, but there was more to it than that. She was . . .

Yolande was not her, never would be. And that was not a crime.

To each his own.

Yolande stirred, began to rock again. "Please, tell me you got rid of that *Messenger*," she whispered.

"I did," replied Savannah. "I did."

Yolande began to weep again.

"It's all over now, Yolande. You really have nothing to fear."

Weeping welled into sobbing. Yolande banged the wall. "Life is not supposed to be like this! At first just a few bombs, then more and more, and now the Pinchbacks . . ."

"True, Yolande. The world is not as it ought to be."

"Not for *us*! These kinds of things don't happen to people

like us! We're supposed to be safe! What if the bombs come here?!"

Is anyone, anywhere safe?

"What if old man Boudinot is a socialist or a Red? What if they come for him next? What if they think everyone on our block is un-American?"

Savannah started to tell Yolande that such talk was silly, but then what did she know? These were savage, unpredictable days.

She looked out Yolande's window, wondered in what part of the yard behind that Tudor-like townhouse Father and Mr. Holloway buried Sebastian. She prayed to God that Yolande had heard wrong. That it was all a mistake. A colossal mistake. And that Marvin and Mildred Pinchback would soon be back in their home.

"Or what if old man Boudinot is a spy?" whimpered Yolande.

Savannah whipped around, saw Yolande sitting up, rubbing her eyes.

"One of our teachers is," Yolande whispered.

SCRAMBLED EGGS AND TOAST

Yolande was grateful when Savannah insisted that they walk to, from school together again.

All the way there the day after the Pinchbacks were dragged from their home, Yolande walked with her head down, stomach in knots, queasy. If only her mother hadn't forced her to eat some of the scrambled eggs on her plate and take a few bites of toast.

At Dunbar Yolande was overwhelmed, at times felt paralyzed by all the whispers.

Edna Fitzhugh said that Latin teacher Mr. Groves had been arrested. So had one of the home economics teachers, Flemmie Castell.

Theophilus Graham said *three* teachers at Armstrong were arrested. "Around midnight, dragged out in pajamas and nightgowns."

Yolande couldn't concentrate, focus during classes. Between one class and another she hurried to a bathroom, almost didn't make it to the sink before the scrambled eggs and toast came up.

AS IT OUGHT TO BE

When Savannah found Yolande balled up and sobbing in a bathroom stall, she didn't know what to do, felt useless, helpless.

"Come, Yolande, let me take you down to Miss Ames," she finally said. "She can see if you're running a fever, maybe give you an aspirin, or set up a cot and let you take a nap."

Yolande shook her head. "No nurse. No nobody. I just want—"

"Want what?"

"It's all so horrible! Things are supposed to be *better* now. Everything is falling apart. Everything is going *wrong*."

There has never been a time when there wasn't misery in the world somewhere.

Yolande stamped her foot. "I just want things *normal*!"

"Want me to ask the principal to call your mother?"

Savannah could see that Yolande was trying to compose herself.

"No."

"Think you can make it through the school day?"

Yolande nodded. "I'll try."

Savannah was proud of Yolande for making it through. "What do you say to Board's?" she asked as they stepped through Dunbar's outer doors.

Yolande shook her head. "No. I just want to go home."

During a silent walk, something Yolande said kept ringing in Savannah's head.

I just want things normal!

For them normal was a nice home, plenty to eat, the latest clothes, Highland Beach, money to spare for sundaes and photoplays.

For alley dwellers, normal was a hovel for a home, soot and filth, getting by with chamber pots, kerosene lamps, and candles, fending off rats.

For Lloyd's friend Spencer, normal was toiling away at the Navy Yard with an improperly healed back.

By the time the girls reached home, the words of Hubert H. Harrison were once again crowding out other thoughts.

The world, as it ought to be . . .

EVIL UNLOOSED

There was soon more reason to weep and fear.

Negro veteran, Negro woman strung up outside Pickens, Mississippi.

Near Dublin, Georgia, a Negro man snatched from police custody, tied with his back to a tree, then "shot to pieces." This after he supposedly fessed up to assaulting a white girl.

Negro man, a former soldier, burned alive near El Dorado, Arkansas.

Near Eatonton, Georgia, a Negro lodge hall, two schools, five churches made ashes.

And yet, after so much evil unloosed . . .

On Decoration Day, the day after a total eclipse of the sun—six minutes, newspapers predicted, but invisible to DC eyes—Father, like Oscar Holloway, like old man Boudinot, like other men on the block, hung an American flag outside their home. The only house without one was the Pinchbacks' with its still boarded-up front door.

Three days later Savannah thought herself in a nightmare.

Clap of thunder?

Cannon boom?

Sky raining glass?

She sat bolt upright, blinked, blinked again in the darkness.

Father burst into her room, flashlight in hand. "Savannah, come!"

"What's happening?"

The white light was blinding.

"Just come!"

The next thing she knew, Father had her by the arm and was practically dragging her from her bedroom.

Mother on the landing. Two flashlights in hand. Shucking her robe, wrapping it around Savannah, then kicking off her slippers. "You take these."

Dogs howled, sirens wailed.

When they reached the door to the basement, a terrified Savannah was practically screaming, "What's wrong, what's happening?!"

SUNSHINE KRISPY CRACKERS TOO

No lark sparrow trills. No flycatcher whistles. No blue jay whirs and whines. No birdsong at all.

Curtains, drapes of every house—as far she could see from her bedroom balcony, the living room window, the parlor—drawn tight.

God had gone away.

Following a solemn, mostly silent breakfast of hominy, sausage, and eggs, Father had headed out, but not before making a number of telephone calls.

"Do be careful," said Savannah.

"And please don't be out long," added Mother.

Father gently pinched their noses. "No worrying."

Savannah busied herself in the living room. Dusting, tidying, rearranging the brass-cased clock, the bust of Frederick Douglass, the stack of miniature books on the fireplace mantel.

The telephone rang.

She tensed.

"I'll get it!" She hurried to the hallway.

"The Riddle residence . . ." Savannah lit up, clamped her hand over the receiver. "Mother! It's Charlie!"

Back to the call.

"Charlie . . . We don't know . . . Father has gone to . . . What!? . . . Was anyone— . . . Oh, how dreadful!" Hand clamped over the receiver again, Savannah cried out, "Mother! A bomb went off in New York City too!"

From the sound of her footfalls, Mother couldn't get there fast enough.

"Charlie, are you all right? . . . Judge who? . . . Where? . . . How far is that from where you live? . . . You stay close to home today . . . When he returns I'll have him call you."

Yolande, Savannah thought as Mother hung up the phone. "Mother, I'm going next door."

Mrs. Holloway answered.

"I just thought I'd stop by and see how Yolande is doing."

Mrs. Holloway stepped out of the house. "She is not doing well at all," she whispered.

"May I see her?"

"Not now, dear. I've given her something to help her sleep."

A long two hours later, back in her home, perched in her living room's bay window, Savannah sent up a sigh of relief.

There was Father, at last, coming up the walkway heavy-laden with bulging brown paper bags.

"Charlie called. A bomb went off in New York City last night," said Savannah, relieving Father of a bag.

"Is he all right?"

"Yes. It was blocks and blocks away."

Mother prepared another pot of coffee. Savannah began unpacking the food.

Armour corned beef.

Seacrest sardines.

Del Monte white asparagus, spinach, tomatoes.

Victory baked beans.

Bordens's condensed milk.

Campbell's chicken soup.

Campbell's tomato soup.

Campbell's oxtail soup.

Sunshine Krispy crackers too.

Father stood at the kitchen window, hands in trouser pockets, stretching his neck, his back.

"Pumpkin, just leave it all on the counter for now," he said. "Might be best if we store some of it in the basement."

Savannah had rocks in her stomach as she waited for Father to hurry up and tell them what he'd found out. Was the bombing anywhere near his office? Anyone dead? Wounded? Had it—or them—been made to look like a package from Gimbel Brothers?

But Savannah stifled herself, knowing that with Father there was always an order to things.

So she just watched Mother watch the coffeepot percolate.

Watched Father take a seat at the kitchen table.

Watched Father motion her to do likewise.

Watched Mother fill one cup, another cup.

Heard Father say, "Savannah, would you like a cup?"

"Really?" Savannah was exhilarated.

"I think you are old enough," replied Father.

Savannah was also terrified. If they were letting her have coffee, things must be very bad.

"Home of Attorney General Palmer," said Father after his first sip.

"Where's that?" asked Savannah.

"Over in Kalorama. R Street."

"Is he—?"

"Not a scratch, they say. Family's fine too. Assistant Secretary of the Navy Roosevelt and his wife were just arriving home—they live across the street from the Palmers—and they are unharmed too." Father took another sip.

"Front of Palmer's house is near demolished. Some homes nearby, windows shattered, doors blown in." Father rested his cup in its saucer. "Only the bomber died. Blown to butcher's meat. Theory is he tripped going up the walkway." Father swallowed. "Anarchist."

Mother was letting her coffee go cold.

As was Savannah. "How do they know he was an anarchist?"

"Leaflets strewn all over signed 'The Anarchist Fighters.'"

Father pinched the bridge of his nose. He looked so weary. "There were other bombings last night."

"Other than in New York City?" Savannah's stomach was now too sick, too nervous for coffee.

Father nodded. "Home of Cleveland's mayor, a judge in Boston, politician somewhere else in Massachusetts. In Philadelphia a Catholic church rectory, a jeweler's home."

Savannah's eyes wandered over to the counter laden with canned food and Sunshine Krispy crackers as Father added that in Pittsburgh the homes of a judge and some official with immigration had been targeted, and that of a silk manufacturer staunchly opposed to unions in a place in New Jersey she had never heard of, Paterson. "Does Charlie know that in New York it was a judge's home?"

Savannah nodded. "A watchman was killed."

Father took another sip of coffee. "The hunt was on before the break of day. For foreigners mostly."

Savannah prayed that Lloyd kept his head down, had the good sense not to hold any more meetings.

Over dinner, meatloaf and mash, Savannah brought up something that had been gnawing at her for days. Every time she ran into the woman at school she avoided her gaze.

A woman she had so admired during the war for the work

she did with Howard University's Red Cross unit, who had gone on a fact-finding mission after East Saint Louis, a woman to whom her parents and scores of others in the District had entrusted money raised for the victims.

This brilliant woman fluent in not only Spanish, but also in French and German, who looked *so* angelic, had eyes that brought to mind a poet.

And she wrote for the *Crisis*.

"Miss Queen . . . ?"

"Who?" asked Mother.

"Hallie E. Queen, one of our Spanish teachers."

"What about her?" asked Father, queer glance at Mother.

Savannah swallowed. "Is she a spy?"

"Where did you hear that?" asked Mother.

"Yolande."

Father bit the inside of his lip, winced. "We have heard of this."

"Do you believe it?"

Mother began wringing her hands. "Sometimes patriotism can make people do strange things."

"Fear will do that too," added Father.

"You think she *willingly* spied on her own people? Maybe the government made her do it—maybe they had something on her. Or maybe . . ."

"Savannah," said Mother, "let us never speak of this again."

"And you must promise me," added Father, "that you will *never* mention it to another living soul. I advise you tell Yolande—never mind, I'll have a word with Oscar."

Had it been silly, baseless gossip her parents would have said so flat-out.

"And there's something else that you should know, Savannah." Father reached for her hand, squeezed it. "Marvin—Mr. Pinchback, he was found hanged in his cell a few days ago."

Tears rolled down Savannah's cheeks.

"They say there's an investigation under way."

"And Mrs. Pinchback?" Savannah wiped her eyes.

"She's to be released in a few days. They say she will sell the house and move to Philadelphia where her sister lives."

The paper boy came late.

"BOMB AT ATTORNEY GENERAL'S HOME STARTS A NATION-WIDE ROUND-UP OF ANARCHISTS" announced page one of the *Star*.

Rattled by the photograph of the wreckage, rattled by the certainty that the beautiful Hallie E. Queen was a spy, by Mr. Pinchback's death, and Mrs. Pinchback's unimaginable grief, Savannah let her eyes drift up to the box to the left of the masthead with the subhead "WEATHER."

"Fair, continued warm tonight; tomorrow unsettled and . . ."

Two days later, given the doubts Lloyd had seeded, Savannah was betwixt and between on how to feel about news that had

Mother buzzing all afternoon—receiving telephone calls, making telephone calls, proclaiming, "Glory to God!"

Page three of the June fifth *Star* chose the following headline for the news: "WOMAN SUFFRAGE WINS IN SENATE."

CRAB PUFFS FOR YOLANDE

For Savannah there was no going out to Lincoln Heights for a while. And that she understood.

What she couldn't fathom, what frightened, unnerved her was that Yolande never returned to Dunbar for the remaining few days of school.

She didn't go to church either.

Weekday mornings there was Yolande looking out her bedroom window. Still in nightclothes, she gave Savannah a limp wave or looked right through her.

"She's resting," said Mrs. Holloway on weekday afternoons, weekends too.

Savannah thought back to when she was trapped in a maze of melancholy. She had been able to leave the house, keep up her grades, pack comfort kits.

"It's been days and days," Savannah despaired as she and Mother stood in their kitchen making crab puffs for Yolande.

What Savannah would give to hear her friend prattle on and on about a party or anything else.

Chatter that would take Savannah's mind off news about

whether enough states would ratify the Anthony amendment, news about whitefolks in the South raising a hue and cry about Negro woman suffrage. And there was news with headlines like "THREE RADICALS TAKEN IN RAID BY DISTRICT POLICE."

News too of more race riots.

After the one in Annapolis, her parents decided against that annual vacation in Highland Beach.

"Best we stay close to home," said Father.

Is anyone, anywhere safe? Savannah wondered once again.

Not Macon, Mississippi.

Not Bisbee, Arkansas.

Not if you were Negro—poor, rich, high school dropout, college student, veteran, denizen of saloons and pool halls, deacon of a church.

Not in Scranton, Pennsylvania, or Dublin, Georgia, or the City of Brotherly Love or Coatesville, Pennsylvania, Tuscaloosa, Alabama, Longview, Texas, Baltimore, Maryland, Port Arthur, Texas, or . . .

With each account of heaving hatred, of Negro schools, homes, churches, bodies under attack, Savannah clung to something Yolande once said.

Yes, we have to contend with the color line, but the whitefolks here are not nearly so barbaric.

SACHEMS, CABBAGE WHITES, AND TIGER SWALLOWTAILS

As the black Buick pulled off, Savannah just stood there, took a deep breath, then smiled.

At the farm stand's bright green paint.

At its billowing banner, WE SPECIALIZE IN THE WHOLLY IMPOSSIBLE.

Would she ever specialize in anything? If not the wholly impossible, the slightly impossible?

Perhaps start with the possible came a whisper from the wind that blew by bushel baskets overflowing with pole beans and corn and cucumbers and tomatoes and squash—yellow and green—and beets and peppers and heads of lettuce as big as a grown man's head.

"Good morning, Blanche! Good morning, Flossie!"

"Good morning, Savannah!" said the girls in unison, then rushed from behind the stand to give Savannah a long hug.

"Mona told us you called," added Blanche.

Then Flossie, "Welcome back!"

Savannah spotted Mona making her way down.

"Bonjou zanmi! Kijan ou ye?"

"Mwen byen, mési," replied Mona, a muslin sack of coins in one hand, cash box in the other.

Savannah lost no time getting her apron out of her satchel and putting it on over her butterscotch gingham dress, then slipping out of white Nubucks and into Sister Sue white Keds. Out, too, came a straw hat on this day with a sky graced by sachems, cabbage whites, and tiger swallowtails. Savannah felt renewed by the sight of the farm stand, Blanche, Flossie, and Mona's cheer.

And the butterflies.

The girls took turns weighing, bagging, making change, hauling down produce when bushel baskets ceased to over-flow, walking up and down the line advertising prices.

"Lettuce . . . five cents a head! . . . Tomatoes . . . seven cents a pound! And get your string beans . . . six cents a pound! And we have corn and we have peppers and we have beets! Beets just five cents a bunch!"

High noon had come and gone when Savannah spotted Lloyd at the end of the line. She was returning to the stand with a croker sack of tomatoes over one shoulder, a sack of peppers over the other. After refilling bushel baskets she scrunched down behind the stand with her purse, pulled out her compact, checked to make sure no hair was out of place. She then went out front and walked the line.

"Lettuce . . . give five cents a head . . ."

During the intervening days when Miss Gertie came to clean, Savannah had ached to ask about Lloyd, then thought better. Instead she asked, "How's the family?"

"Fine."

"Everyone?"

"Yes."

"Well, well, Miss Ting is back!" His smile so broad.

"Yes, I'm back!" said Savannah, wishing she had the guts to say, "I've missed you!"

"You've just now come to work?" she asked when it registered that Lloyd was in regular street clothes, not work clothes.

"I come for my last pay and some vegetables Auntie asked me to bring, 'cause I told her Principal Burroughs gives me a discount."

Wait a minute. What did he say? "Your final pay?"

Lloyd nodded.

Savannah shifted from foot to foot. "Will you come next week for more produce?" she blurted out before realizing she wasn't scheduled to be out at Lincoln Heights next week. But maybe if he was coming, maybe she'd ask her parents if she could do back-to-back Saturdays out at Lincoln Heights.

Lloyd shook his head. "Next Saturday is a big day. A true

Moses is coming, will deliver a lecture that evening, and I'm the main host."

"Who's this, this Moses?"

"Hubert Harrison."

Savannah gasped. "Really?"

Never, ever had she seen Lloyd shocked. "You heard of him, Miss Ting?"

"When you gave me the *Messenger*, it had a clipping, one of his articles."

"Which one?"

Savannah frowned. "I don't remember the title, only that it had 'New Negro' in it."

"That could be any one of his articles." Lloyd jingled coins in a trouser pocket. "Enjoyed it?"

"What?"

"The Harrison piece."

"Oh, most definitely. It was—"

"You want to attend the lecture?"

"What time?"

"Starts at seven o'clock."

"Where?"

"Southwest."

Savannah bit her lip as she thought. Then a light bulb beamed in her head. "Yes, I can. I can be there."

"Meet at the edge of the Capitol lawn?"

BECKONED BY THE PAST

Savannah had the perfect plan.

Once her parents left for the Lees' dinner party, she'd change, slip out.

Lloyd said everything would likely be over by nine o'clock at the latest. Plenty of time for her to get back home, be in bed when her parents returned at what, about ten thirty, maybe even eleven.

And it all went off without a hitch. Her parents even left a little early.

In a flash Savannah was out of her yellow cotton house-dress and into a linen skirt, white blouse, white hose, white kidskin rubber-heeled shoes. Topping it off, a simple cream silk-and-cotton short-brimmed hat with a lavender ribbon around the crown. With off-white needle-lace gloves on her hands and a linen drawstring purse dangling from a wrist, by five thirty p.m., Savannah was out the door and into the evening's steamy heat.

She slowed her pace, did her best to look nonchalant as

she neared the edge of the Capitol lawn where Lloyd was
waiting.

It had to be hovering around 100 degrees.

No surprise. It was July after all. The city's swampland
history making itself known.

And in the shadow of the Capitol, Savannah was beckoned by the past.

For the first time, thinking of the souls who may have
paved the street beneath her feet.

Back to men, perhaps named George, Enoch, Harry, Luke,
and such, hauling stone quarried with pickaxes and mauls in
Virginia, while others, perhaps named Ben, Daniel, Samuel,
Elijah, Peter, Paul—carpenters, joiners, masons—giving shape,
form, substance to an architect's dream of the Capitol, of the
president's house.

Were there Hannahs and Sarahs and Annies on the scene?
Drawers of water? Cooks for building crews?

Savannah racked her brains for another name that wasn't
a perhaps.

Musician born free in New York, lured to the capital with
the promise of work, only to end up scourged and chained
in the Yellow House, then made cargo to Louisiana, where he
endured twelve long years a slave.

Years back, during research for an essay, Savannah had
read a white abolitionist's account of his visit to a slave pen.

Cruel, cramped place. Men, women, children, babies sweltered in the summer. Some froze to death in winter. The sole small window unglazed.

Something about this steaming July evening . . .

Savannah found it increasingly unnerving.

The heavy air, the heat. Haunted by distant screams, pleas of children, families, all-alone women on auction blocks as senators and society ladies strolled by.

Savannah glanced around as she and Lloyd walked on. Not a soul seemed fazed by the past.

Crowds of people out. Couples strolling hand in hand. Families. Best friends. Going to, from theaters, posh restaurants, cafés with gingham curtains. People sat on stoops with wet towels around their necks, their heads.

When they neared a crowd of kids around a hokey-pokey man's horse-drawn cart, Lloyd stopped. "Do you want one?"

"Why, yes, thank you. Lemon, please."

When Lloyd stepped away from the cart with but a single paper cup—

"You didn't want one?"

Lloyd shook his head. "Not big on sweets."

Gloves off and tucked into her purse, Savannah took the lemon ice from Lloyd's hand, a hand part of her ached to hold again.

She stole glances at Lloyd as she licked her lemon ice. As at Nannie Burroughs's lecture, he wore a brown sack suit. Same blue-and-white-striped club collar shirt. Same skinny knit tie. Same brown cap toe shoes. Same Knox felt hat. She reckoned this was Lloyd's only nice outfit. And she wondered.

Surely, he'd be more than a mechanic and catch-as-catch-can laborer had he been born a Sanderson, a Holloway, a Riddle? Would he soon be a graduate of Amherst or Howard or Oberlin? Poised to start an insurance company or real estate agency? Maybe envisioning his own high-class hotel?

Or maybe he would have been like Charlie. Left Amherst or Howard or Oberlin after a year and followed his own mind.

"Lloyd?"

"Yeah."

"What made you leave Saint Thomas? Why did you come here?"

"Wanted to live."

"What?"

"Ran afoul of authorities."

Savannah swallowed, then plowed on. "Ran afoul how?—if you don't mind my asking?"

"Speeches. Meetings. They said I was stirring up the masses, branded me a troublemaker. One night, five, six policemen grab me up, take me out to a cane field, told me I had two choices."

Heart in her mouth, Savannah stopped licking her lemon ice.

"I could get beat to a pulp, left for dead, or—"

"Go."

"And never, ever return." Lloyd's eyes were on the ground.

And Savannah's were on him until swiftly, but gently, he steered her to the doorway of a dry goods store.

A pack of stumbling-drunk white sailors barreled by.

"Disgusting," she muttered.

"If the congressman—name escapes me—the one who a few weeks back introduced a bill on enforcement of the Prohibition amendment—"

"Volstead," said Savannah.

"Yeah, Volstead. If the bill succeed, streets will be free of such foolishness."

The sight of those sailors brought to mind the men who dragged the Pinchbacks from their home.

Savannah told Lloyd about that awful day, down to little Sebastian's weak whimpers. "You must be careful, Lloyd!"

She also told him of how her family spent that frightening night when Attorney General Palmer's home—like other homes, other places—was bombed.

"And you, Miss Ting, you must be brave. Everybody gotta be real brave."

"And all these riots . . ."

"Poisons hatching out, Miss Ting. Poisons hatching out."

AREOPAGITICA

The lecture was held in a fairly large room of a basement apartment.

Packed.

Most of the men in sack suits, some fiddling with flat caps, fedoras in calloused hands, hands with swollen knuckles.

Women—cleaners, cooks, washerwomen, likely, along with a shopgirl or two—were in what Savannah took to be their Sunday best.

Seated on neatly placed wooden folding chairs, people chatted, read pamphlets, fanned. Others milled around a camping table covered with a white cloth and laid with small paper cups of water and a tray with squares of pound cake.

Lloyd escorted Savannah to a front seat.

"Oh, no, I don't want to—"

"Front row seat, Miss Ting." He laid his hat on a seat beside her. "It won't be long now," he said, then headed for a closed door.

Savannah literally twiddled her fingers as she waited, picking up snatches of conversations.

"Weekend couldn't come soon enough."

"Yuh boy still searching for work?"

"Miss Haysmith back in de hospital."

West Indian. Almost all.

Then came a tap on her shoulder. Savannah turned.

"Name's Glenna." A young woman leaned forward, held out her hand.

"Savannah."

"You not from around here?"

"I don't live that far away."

"How do you know Lloyd?"

Now Savannah took a good look at the young woman.

Pretty. Big-boned with deep-set eyes. She didn't quite sound like Lloyd. More singsong in her voice.

What's it to her how I know Lloyd?

"I've known the family for years," Savannah replied.

Thanks goodness! Lloyd came through the door with a glass of water in one hand, and Glenna sat back in her seat.

Lloyd rested the glass on the podium, brought out a piece of paper from his pocket, cleared his throat.

Hubbub ceased. And Savannah savored the sight of him.

"Brothers and sisters," Lloyd began. "This evening I have the distinct honor of introducing a true Moses, a man born at the bottom in Saint Croix, a man who through mighty force of will trained his mind by reading every newspaper, magazine, every book he put his hands on, a man who talks just as deep about *Alice in Wonderland* as he talks about the German philosopher Immanuel Kant."

Lloyd knows of Kant?

"And this man, one of this new era's fiercest champions of the Negro people, he comes with the same spirit of the Crucian brothers and sisters who led the great uprising of 1848. He comes with the spirit of the Crucian brothers and sisters who rallied up people for the great Fireburn of 1878. Brothers and sisters, I present you Hubert Henry Harrison."

Amid fervent applause, a dark-skinned shortish stocky man stepped through the door. Full lips. Full nose. Huge, bulging head. Savannah saw a boxer determined to defeat every foe.

Reaching the podium, Harrison shook hands with Lloyd, then Lloyd took his seat beside Savannah.

"Thank you, Brother Lloyd. And I thank all of you for the fine welcome," said Harrison. "You to whom I bring greetings from comrades in Harlem."

He took a sip of water.

"Tonight I want to speak to you on what I call our larger duty." He cleared his throat. "The problem of the twentieth century is the problem of the color line."

"Fuh true, fuh true!" a man shouted.

Harrison smiled. "But what is the color line?"

"Hell from the devil!" That was Glenna.

Harrison nodded. "It is the practice of the theory that the colored and supposed other weaker races of the earth shall not be free to follow their own way of life, but shall *live, work* and *be governed* as the dominant white race may decide."

His diction so precise, biting. His voice a martial song.

"Consider for a moment the full meaning of this fact. Of

the seventeen hundred million people that dwell on our earth today *more than twelve hundred million* are colored—black and brown and . . . not white at all."

He paused, small, intense eyes afire, brow glistening with sweat.

"Let me say that again: Of the seventeen hundred million people that dwell on our earth today, *twelve hundred million* are colored."

"So you mean there is only five hundred million white people?" a man asked. Savannah looked back to see the speaker was an elderly man clutching a handmade cane. In his cloudy eyes, his wrinkled skin, those gnarled hands clutching that cane, Savannah saw a thousand sorrows borne.

Harrison nodded, smiled, pointed to the elderly man. "Is everyone in the capital as smart as this group?"

Giggles, chortles, guffaws. When the crowd settled into silence—

"The so-called white race is, of course, the superior one. That is to say, it is on top by virtue of its control of the physical force of the world—*ships, guns, soldiers, money*. By virtue of this control, England rules and robs India, Egypt, Africa, and the West Indies. By virtue of this control, the United States can tell Haitians, Hawaiians, and Filipinos how much they shall get for their labor and what shall be done in their lands. By virtue of this control, Belgium can still say to the Congolese whether they shall have their hands hacked off or their eyes gouged out."

Harrison whipped out a handkerchief, mopped his gleaming brow.

"It is thus clear that, as long as the color line exists, all the perfumed protestations of Democracy on the part of the white race must be simply downright *lying*!"

The crowd erupted into applause.

Joining in with gusto, Savannah thought, *How plainly, wonderfully put. Downright lying. "Sweet Land of Liberty"— Another lie!*

Coins she and others carried in pockets and purses—

Ten-cent piece: Winged *Liberty*.

Twenty-five-cent piece: Standing *Liberty*.

Fifty-cent piece: Walking *Liberty*.

Downright lying!

As for the five-cent piece . . . On one side a buffalo. On the other, in profile, a stoic-looking Indian man with a weathered face.

Was the buffalo nickel an apology or a boast?

"The hypocritical talk of 'Democracy,'" Harrison bellowed, "is intended as dust in the eyes of white voters, incense on the altar of their own self-love. The good news?"

During the pause, like others, Savannah leaned forward.

"Colored people around the world have taken the measure of this cant and hypocrisy. And whatever the white world may think, it will have these peoples to deal with during this twentieth century."

More applause.

Savannah was seeing such a wider world as Harrison spoke of movements for liberty on the rise, his emphasis on Africa, speaking of the Ethiopian Movement, of Zulus, of the Ekoi of Nigeria.

She could listen to Harrison all day, all night.

"In short, the darker races, chafing under the domination of the alien white, are everywhere showing a disposition to take Democracy at its word and to win some measure of it—for themselves!"

More applause.

"For *themselves*!" Harrison banged his fist on the podium. The water in his glass trembled.

Over her shoulder Savannah saw tears streaming down that elderly man's face.

Harrison looked out over the audience. "What part in this great drama of the future are the Negroes of the Western world to play?"

He let the question hang in the air.

What part might I *play in this great drama?* wondered Savannah. *What is* my *reason for being?*

Harrison called on the crowd to stay informed about movements for freedom, for true democracy around the world, to be in solidarity with the oppressed and downtrodden *everywhere*.

"Africa! Africa! Africa!" he cried out. "So will we profit by a wider experience and perhaps be able to lend some assistance to that ancient Mother Land of ours to whom we may fittingly apply the words of Milton."

Eyes closed, arms outstretched, Hubert Henry Harrison spoke now in the softest of voices.

"'Methinks I see in my mind a noble and puissant nation rousing herself like a strong man after sleep . . .'"

It struck a chord.

"'And shaking her invincible locks . . .'"

It triggered a memory.

"'Methinks I see her as an eagle mewing her mighty youth, and kindling her undazzled eyes at the full noon-day beam . . .'"

As Harrison rolled on, Savannah mouthed words memorized two, three years ago, meaningless then. And she had had to look up "puissant."

Powerful.

The crowd was on its feet.

"'. . . while the whole noise of timorous and flocking birds, with those also that love the twilight, flutter about, amazed at what she means . . .'"

The applause, the cheering drowned out the rest of Harrison's recitation of *Areopagitica*.

"A-re-o-pa-*git*-i-ka—Remember soft 'g.'" Dunbar's nasally Mr. Neval had said when he assigned that piece of prose. "The title derives from ancient Greece's Areopagus, a hill in Athens where judges once ruled, where a sage urged reform, where the Apostle Paul preached."

During the hope-spawned applause, Lloyd returned to the podium. He and Harrison embraced, then Lloyd turned to the audience, motioned for folks to settle down. Room quiet, Lloyd beckoned for someone to come forward.

Spencer with the bent back. He made his way to the front with a cut-glass punch bowl.

"Brothers and Sisters," said Lloyd, "you know talk really is not cheap, not good talk like what Brother Hubert Henry Harrison provide. So we ask you to search your hearts, be as generous as you can."

Spencer began to walk the rows with the punch bowl.

Savannah opened her purse, reached for two dollar bills, paused, looked around. She saw only coins being dropped into the punch bowl.

You not from around here?

From her change purse Savannah brought out a Walking Liberty.

"No matter how much you are able to give," said Lloyd, "when you exit, help yourself to a copy of the latest issue of a magazine Harrison associates with, *The New Negro*. You'll also find some pamphlets by another Moses, Marcus Mosiah Garvey."

By the time Savannah made her way through the crowd to the camping table, all the pound cake was gone. But she didn't care. She wasn't there for cake, but to shake Mr. Harrison's hand.

"I just want to thank you, sir. You really have me thinking!"

"It is what I live for. And you, I saw you reciting *Areopagitica* along with me."

"I had to memorize it for a school program. But I never *felt* the words until tonight." Savannah made a cat's cradle of her hands as she floundered for something more to say.

Then this. "My brother, he lives in Harlem."

"Does he, now?"

"Yes, on 135th Street. His name is Charlie Riddle."

Harrison smiled. "The photographer?"

Savannah nodded rapidly. "Yes, that's him."

Harrison was still smiling. "He's covered some Liberty League events."

As soon as Savannah got home, she'd telephone Charlie, tell him that she'd met Harrison and pepper him with questions about the Liberty League. She had to know more.

Savannah took a quick peek at her bracelet watch. "Mr. Harrison, sir, I must be going. And, again, thank you for a stirring, riveting, and most puissant speech, for such a—for such an awakening."

Harrison responded with a slight bow.

Savannah looked around for Lloyd, spotted him in a corner talking with Glenna.

She hurried over. "Excuse me, Glenna, I just need a word with Lloyd."

Once they were off to the side, Savannah pointed at her watch. "It's after *nine*."

"Right," said Lloyd. "Just a few more minutes. We're waiting for a buddy who's to drive Harrison to his lodgings for the night. I want to see him off."

As minutes ticked by, Savannah grew increasingly antsy. She *had* to get home before her parents. If she didn't—

Her plan was falling apart.

Finally Lloyd's buddy came, he saw Harrison off, and they were on their way.

The night was even steamier. Not a breeze to be had.

"Thanks for tonight," said Savannah. "I wouldn't have missed this for the world." She had them walking fast-fast. "Mr. Harrison has me dreaming of seeing the pyramids, of learning more about Zulus and the—"

"The Ekoi."

"Right, the Ekoi."

They walked for a while in silence.

"I've never really thought . . ."

"Thought what?"

"About the world. Not the way he spoke of it. Never thought that I might have something in common with, say, a girl in India or in—"

Commotion up ahead.

Cursing, shouting, feet running hard, fast.

A shatter of glass.

Savannah and Lloyd stopped.

The trouble was coming their way.

A bloodied Negro man rounded the corner followed by another, his shirt halfway ripped off.

Hard on their heels a sea of white men.

People scattered.

The next thing Savannah knew, Lloyd snatched her into a crevice of an alley. It reeked of piss and beer and vomit.

Back against the wall, frightened out of her mind, Savannah did her best to hold her breath.

More feet pounding pavement was coming their way.

White men passed by as if marching off to war. Savannah saw hands clutching knives, cudgels, sticks, bricks. One man banged a drum. Many, she could tell from carriage and gait, were drunk.

Some in sailor suits.

Others in khaki and olive drab.

They were shouting out a name, sounded like "Walls."

Windows smashed.

Shots rang out.

Not far away a sickening chant.

Eeny, meeny, miny, moe!
Catch a—

Tears burned down Savannah's face.

If he hollers, cut his throat!
Eeny, meeny, miny, moe!

Chaos owned the night.

Savannah looked to her right.

Nothing but pitch black.

She tried not to tremble, tried to stop the tears. Something skittered past her feet.

Eeny, meeny, miny, moe!
Catch a—

But the tears wouldn't cease.

If he hollers, cut his throat!
Eeny, meeny, miny, moe!

From near and far Savannah heard voices—men, women—crying out for mercy, heard bloodcurdling screams, smelled burning.

Lloyd eased down to the ground. When he rose, she made out that he had a brick or a stone or something in one hand and in the other—

He handed her a lead pipe. Her stomach churned and lurched.

The chanting was drowned out by cries and shouts, howls, rebel yells, more banging of pots and pans.

Cacophony from hell.

Savannah clamped a hand over her mouth as tears continued down her cheeks, hoping, praying.

Soon, the clamor grew fainter, fainter, a wave rolling out to sea.

Is this happening all over? Savannah was stiff with panic.

What time is it?

Are Mother and Father safe? At the Lees'? At home?

Mother says thank heavens we live in the capital . . . white-folks here are not nearly so barbaric.

The lull didn't last.

Again feet pounding the cobblestone street were coming their way.

Savannah shut tight her eyes.

Every second an eternity.

As the feet passed by that crevice of an alley, Lloyd took her hand. "Come."

"But—"

As a trembling Savannah inched out into the street, grateful tears streamed down her face.

Those feet belonged to Negro men. Men with bludgeons, blackjacks, crowbars. Some had pistols, rifles. Spencer was among them.

"Wha going on, fellas?" Lloyd called out.

The men stopped, turned.

When Lloyd and Savannah reached them, Spencer spoke.

"Last night, some white woman claimed two Negro men accosted her, tried to take her umbrella. Husband is a navy man. Last night there was rumblings, but they calmed down when word spread the police had two Negro men in lockup. Then today they found out they was released."

Savannah stepped over to a streetlamp, checked her watch.

Ten o'clock.

"We'll see you and the young lady to your door," said Spencer.

"Come on, Savannah," said Lloyd. "It's safest if you stay by us."

"But my parents? I have to know if—" She turned to Spencer. "Any rioting in Northwest?"

"Some trouble I think," he replied. "Not so bad as here."

"I have to call my parents!"

Savannah could see Lloyd thinking fast.

"Spencer, Mr. Fletcher, he has a telephone, right?"

Spencer nodded.

"Joe, Jack, Reuben, Willie, Junius, Jake, come with us, please," said Lloyd.

Savannah noticed that all the men Lloyd summoned had guns.

FRANKLIN 3159

Upstairs, downstairs dark.

Lloyd banged on the door, stepped back, looked up.

An upstairs light went on.

"Mr. Fletcher, it's me, Lloyd Walcott. Your telephone. I need it."

A head poked out a window. "Be right down."

Soon lights went on downstairs, the door opened.

After everyone poured in, Mr. Fletcher bolted the door. This freckle-faced giant of a man who brought to mind a walrus was wearing an undershirt and white duck trousers held up by a suspender strap.

"Your telephone, sir?" asked Savannah, eyeing the shotgun in Mr. Fletcher's hand.

"Back there on the counter."

"Yes, Operator, Franklin 3159."

Ring.

Ring.

Ring.

Through a new trickle of tears, Savannah stared at shelves packed with sardines and other tinned goods, at a short counter with giant jars of pickled pigs' feet.

After what seemed the hundredth ring, she hung up the telephone, felt about to faint.

"Where she live exactly?" asked Spencer.

"M Street Northwest. 900 block."

Spencer frowned. "I don't think we chance it. Best she stay by you."

Lloyd nodded.

"Please!" Savannah cried out. "Just give me a few more minutes, *please!* Let me try again! *Please!*"

A squat woman in a blue-check bungalow dress entered through a curtain behind the main counter. After one look at Savannah, she made an about-face. Seconds later the woman reappeared, damp cloth in one hand, a glass of water in the other. "Here ya go, dearie." She scurried back behind the curtain.

Savannah wiped her face, but she couldn't get the stench of that crevice of an alley out of her nostrils. After gulping down the water, her breathing slowed.

"Mr. Fletcher," said Spencer with a nod at a jar of pickled pigs' feet. "One, please." He fished in his pocket.

"On me, son," said Mr. Fletcher, unscrewing the jar. From beneath the counter he brought out a sheet of wax paper and a long two-pronged fork. He speared a pig foot, held it over the jar, let it drip. After a tick of time he wrapped the pig foot in the wax paper, handed it to Spencer. "The rest of you boys?" asked Mr. Fletcher.

Joe, Jack, Reuben, and the others lined up at the short counter.

But not Lloyd. He just stared at Savannah.

She stared back, then reached for the receiver again, gave the operator her exchange and number again.

Ring. Ring. Ring. Ri—

"Father! Are you and Mother all right? . . . I'm sorry, I'm sorry, but I'm fine . . . I went to a lecture . . . Lloyd Walcott . . . A grocery store . . . I don't know where I am . . . Southwest . . . We're with some men . . . Protection . . ." She cupped her hand over the receiver. "What's the address here?"

"Lemme speak with him." Lloyd took the phone.

"Lloyd here, Mister Riddle . . . Right now? . . . You got guns? . . . Unless you come with a posse I don't think . . . Men with us now will see us to my house . . . Hello, you still there, Mister Riddle? . . . Mister Riddle? . . . In the morning . . . Right."

"But—" Savannah called out.

"Yeah, Savannah?"

Savannah shook her head. "Never mind." She wanted nothing more than to be *home, in her bed*, but then across her mental sky came that bloodied man rounding that corner, followd by another, his shirt halfway torn off. She'd never forgive herself if something happened to Father while trying to save her from Southwest.

Lloyd handed the phone to Savannah.

"Yes, Father . . . Yes . . . Yes, I feel very safe . . . Okay . . . I love you."

She hung up the phone. "Thank you ever so much, Mr. Fletcher." She turned to Spencer and the other men. "And I thank all of you for giving me a chance to—"

"Riddle?" asked Mr. Fletcher. "You Wyatt Riddle's girl?"

"Yes, sir."

"He's a good man. I'm a customer."

"Thank you, sir, again—and the woman who gave me a cloth, the glass of water, is that your Missus?"

Mr. Fletcher nodded.

"Please thank her too."

FLATIRONS, EVEN

Night air a touch cooler.

Eerie sounds in the distance.

Street after street, stepping over, around broken glass, bricks, stones, pools of blood by moonlight and Millet post streetlamps, a dazed Savannah was spellbound by the sight of safety all around.

Revolvers.

Machetes.

Shovels, wrenches, claw hammers, flatirons, even.

Methinks I see in my mind a noble and puissant nation rousing . . .

Some men stood in doorways, on stoops.

. . . like a strong man after sleep . . .

Others paced rooftops with rifles, sawed-off shotguns.

. . . shaking her invincible locks . . .

Looking around in utter awe and astonishment at these men—

Hell Fighters.

The steady, strong strides of Joe, Jack, Reuben, Willie, Junius, Jake. Of Lloyd—

My Hell Fighters.

All this because some white woman said two Negroes tried to take her umbrella?

Smoldering embers of anger coupled with a pride in a wider world of her people conquered fear.

And Savannah suddenly remembered something, realized that it wasn't just the white mobs to blame.

There had been a recent rise in articles about Negro crimes and alleged crimes in certain newspapers.

"POLICEMAN BATTLES WITH CRAZED NEGRO."

"POSSES SEEK NEGRO WHO ATTACKED GIRL."

And there were items warning white women to stay clear of Negro men, items urging white women to buy police whistles.

And how many of those white women giving in to fear and loathing of Negro men were champing at the bit for more of their own kind to have the vote?

"NEGRO ROUND-UP WILL CONTINUE."

Methinks I see in my mind—

Savannah tightened her grip on that lead pipe just as they turned onto the Walcotts' block, where she was brought up short—they all were—by moaning, groaning.

Balled up between two dented trash cans was a small figure.

"Mister Walcott . . . Miss . . . Fine Lady."

MEWING HER MIGHTY YOUTH

Bim had a swollen right eye, a busted lip, was clutching his right foot. There was blood around him.

Embers of rage flared into a flame as Savannah cradled Bim in her arms. That's when she felt a knot on his head.

"Hold back a minute, Savannah," said Lloyd.

He ran his hands inside Bim's clothes.

"Not his blood." He picked up Bim.

Methinks I see her as an eagle mewing her mighty youth . . .

"Ever grateful, fellas," said Lloyd when they reached his building.

A head popped out from an upstairs window. Nella. "Lloyd, that you?"

"Yeah."

"Thank God!"

In a flash Nella was downstairs, flinging open the door. Her hands flew to her face at the sight of Bim. "Dear Lord."

Then—

"Miss Riddle, what are you doing here?"

METHINKS I SEE

"Auntie, a hot bath please."

Tight-lipped Miss Gertie placed a blanket on the cot.

Lloyd laid Bim down. "And, Auntie, you got Epsom salts?"

Miss Gertie nodded, then rushed down the hall.

Nella put on the kettle.

A dazed Bim moaned. Savannah watched as Lloyd gingerly removed his shoes, socks. The boy's right ankle joint was horribly swollen.

From the back of the apartment Savannah heard water running.

Nella soon brought over a basin of warm water and some rags.

"Let me," said Savannah.

She plunged the rag into the water, wrung it out. Gently she dabbed Bim's cheeks, forehead, mouth, his eye, his blood-stained hands.

"Lloyd, can I see you a minute in the back," she heard Nella say.

Savannah could tell Nella was fussing but couldn't make out her words.

Miss Gertie handed Savannah a cup of ginger tea. "This will help with the pain."

Savannah had just gotten Bim to take a few sips when Lloyd and Nella returned. Lloyd stepped over, scooped up Bim.

Miss Gertie was soon nearby with a bundle. Out came an old bedsheet. She began turning it into bandages. When done she laid the strips of cotton at the foot of the cot.

As Savannah, Nella, Miss Gertie sat around the table in the middle of the room sipping ginger tea, Savannah imagined that Lloyd had ever so gently removed Bim's clothes, then eased him into the Epsom-salted water.

Miss Gertie left the room again.

When her mother was out of range, Nella whispered, "I'm so, so sorry, Miss Riddle. "

"Please, Nella, *just* Savannah. I'm not your mistress. I'm your cousin's friend. And yours."

"Well, I'm sorry that Lloyd took you to that lecture. If it wasn't for him, you would be safe in your home."

"I feel safe here," Savannah whispered. Only then did she notice the dirt and bloodstains on the bottom of her skirt, the rips and stains on her blouse. And that her silk-and-cotton short-brimmed hat, her drawstring purse—gone.

The hat. Left at Mr. Fletcher's store?

The purse. Dropped in that crevice of an alley?

Handkerchief, compact, money, keys, needle-lace gloves, the purse itself. It could all be so easily replaced. So could her hat.

"You must know Mummy and I have *nothing* to do with Lloyd's politics," said Nella. After a pause she added, "Mummy, she really need the work."

Mind on A-re-o-pa-*git*-i-ka, Savannah found Nella a little annoying. *What is she going on about?*

"I will give you a clean-clean nightgown of mine and you can sleep in my bed."

Lloyd returned with Bim in a nightshirt, laid him on the cot.

"Sleep is the last thing on my mind," Savannah told Nella. "I want to sit up with Bim."

Miss Gertie returned, handed Lloyd a jar of black stuff. The label—IODEX—didn't ring a bell. Some kind of ointment, she guessed.

Lloyd drew the curtain around the cot.

After Gertie and Nella retired, after Lloyd fixed himself a pallet on the floor, Savannah sat in that old broad-back mahogany-and-cane armchair.

Watching over Bim.

Reliving every second in that crevice of an alley.

Reliving that cacophony from hell.

The lull, then the sight of all those Hell Fighters.

When Bim, ankle bound up, moaned, she stroked his brow. When he kicked off the coverlet with his good leg, she pulled it up.

Methinks I see in my mind . . .

What part in this great drama of the future are the Negroes of the Western world to play?

Savannah gazed at the moon, at the stars watching over Bim too.

WIDER BAND OF BLUE

Savannah awoke to red, yellow bands of light layered beneath a wider band of blue.

Later, after washing up, neatening her hair, she slipped into a dress of Nella's a size too big, then shared a small breakfast with the Walcotts: a fried egg and a bready thing, a cross between a doughnut and a biscuit. Savannah had never tasted anything like it. And it tasted so good.

After Miss Gertie shooed her away from clearing the breakfast things, Savannah marveled at how peacefully Bim slept.

Arms wrapped around herself, Savannah stepped over to the window.

Not too many bricks and stones littering the street. As far as she could see no streetlight busted. Whose blood was it that surrounded Bim last night? Had he been attacked on this block? Somewhere else? How far did he hobble or crawl before he collapsed a few feet away from the Walcotts' building?

Savannah leaned out when the black Buick pulled up. When Father got out of the car—

"I'll be right down," she said in a hushed voice.

Then to Lloyd, "Will you bring Bim down, please?"

"For what?"

"He needs a doctor. If his ankle isn't seen to properly he could end up with a limp or something."

Lloyd frowned. "Nella, where's the nearest doctor?"

"Doc Nelson is over on—"

"There are four or five within two blocks of my house," said Savannah as she headed to the front door. "Also the man who serves as secretary and treasurer for my father's firm is a doctor."

Doctors cost money. That's what Nella had said months back. At the time Savannah had just thought, *Well, yes,* as if Nella had said people need air to breathe. Now she understood.

Savannah was almost through the front door when Nella called out, hurried up to her with a brown paper bag. "Your clothes from last night."

EYES FACED FRONT

Calm, steady as she walked down the steps. But at the sight of Father, Savannah began sobbing. She rushed into his arms, hugged him with all her might. "Oh, Father, I am so very sorry!"

"We'll talk about it when we get home."

Savannah turned back to the building, saw Lloyd carrying out Bim, faced Father again, saw his teeth on edge.

"Mr. Riddle," said Lloyd with a nod when he reached the black Buick.

"Lloyd." Mr. Riddle nodded back, his voice like the coming of thunder.

"This boy needs a doctor," Savannah told Father.

She opened the back door.

Lloyd laid Bim on the back seat.

Savannah suddenly became alarmed. "What about his family? They'll be worried sick."

"He live with his grandfather. Nice old man but he bewitch."

"Bewitch?"

Lloyd tapped his temple. "I doubt he even know the boy gone. I'll go round later, explain things."

About to get into the front seat, Savannah stopped. She stepped over to Lloyd, hugged him, kissed him on the cheek.

Father's eyes faced front when she got into the car.

LORD CALVERT STEEL-CUT COFFEE

Emerging from the black Buick, Savannah felt the weight of weary for the first time.

She looked next door, saw Yolande in the window, waved.

Mother flew from the house, gave Savannah a crushing hug. "My dear, dear darling girl."

Hugging Mother back, Savannah burst into tears.

"Who is this?" Mother asked as Father lifted Bim from the back seat.

"I'll explain when we get inside," replied Savannah.

Father took Bim into the living room, laid him on the davenport, then went to the telephone.

"Operator, Main 6060, please . . . Jonah, Wyatt here . . . It's a long story, but I've got a little boy over here who got hurt last night . . . Scrapes and bruises, a knot on his head, but the major thing seems to be a busted ankle, which has been bandaged up . . . Not now . . . Hold on, I'll ask."

"Savannah, was there any vomiting last night?"

Savannah shook her head.

"No vomiting, Jonah . . . Hold on, I'll ask."

"Can the boy walk on the foot at all, Savannah?"

Again Savannah shook her head. "But I don't really know. Lloyd carried him everywhere."

"Jonah, we're not sure . . . Uh-huh . . . Uh-huh . . . Appreciate it." Father hung up the telephone.

Mother held Savannah by the shoulders. "Come, I'll draw you a bath, then you'll take a nap."

"I need to stay with Bim."

"No, you don't," said Father. "I'll sit with him until Dr. Galloway arrives."

Savannah was surprised, shocked really, by the tenderness, expected to get a real dressing-down, thought Mother, especially, would go on and on about . . .

But there was none of that. Just the drawing of a bath, the helping her out of Nella's clothes, the combing out of her hair when she entered her bedroom in her robe.

And when Mother helped her into her bed, she got in too, cradled her in her arms. The last thing Savannah remembered was Mother stroking her face.

There was no one in the living room when Savannah came downstairs in a housedress, her hair in that single thick plait that fell a long ways down her back.

But coming from the kitchen were voices and the aroma of Lord Calvert steel-cut coffee.

"Good day, Dr. Galloway."

"Good day, Savannah."

"Where's Bim?"

"Up in Charlie's room," said Father. "Asleep."

"How is he, Dr. Galloway?"

"Not too bad. I've seen worse," replied the doctor, with his stooped shoulders, handlebar mustache, bald pate save for a few wisps of gray on the sides. "Sprain. Not broken. I've rebound it up with this relatively new type of bandage, more breathable, reduces swelling better. They call it the Ace bandage. And I've given your parents instructions on—"

"What is it that we need to do?" asked Savannah.

Dr. Galloway looked at Mother, Father.

"It's fine, Jonah," said Father. "Tell her what you told us."

Dr. Galloway took a sip of coffee. "First he needs plenty of rest—and feeding. The lad's a little underweight." Dr. Galloway winced. "His people?"

"All he's got is a grandfather," replied Savannah. "And from what I understand, the old man is senile."

Dr. Galloway shook his head. "Pity." He sighed. "For the ankle, keep it elevated."

"Rest, food, elevated," said Savannah.

"Yes, and if he seems in pain you can give him a Bayer, no more than three times a day. And ice the ankle about twenty minutes, every two, three hours until the swelling has gone."

"Place the ice over this Ace thing?"

Dr. Galloway put down his cup. "Come, Savannah, I'll show you how things are to be done."

"Thank you, Dr. Galloway."

They were back downstairs, Savannah handing him his coat and hat, then him picking up his black bag from the telephone table.

Savannah walked him to the front door, watched him proceed down the walkway, readied, steadied herself for a talk she knew was coming.

A WIDER WORLD

With Mother and Father at either end of the kitchen table and her in the middle, Savannah told them how she first came to learn of Hubert Henry Harrison.

His article that moved her, made her think.

How when Lloyd told her about the lecture—

"I just *had* to hear Mr. Harrison. Lloyd didn't drag me there. It was my decision."

She told them, too, how thrilling an experience it had been.

"I know you must have been worried sick last night when you returned home. And I'm sorry about that, but—"

She was reminded of something Nella had said. "And please, know that Miss Gertie and Nella had *nothing* to do with it. They didn't even know I went to the lecture until I turned up at their place."

Savannah rose from the kitchen table, walked over to the window. What she had to say was best said without being eye to eye with her parents.

"I love you so very much, and I know how much you've

done for me, how blessed I am, but the thing is I want a different life from what you want for me."

"And what is it that you think we want for you?" asked Mother.

"A life like yours. Comfortable. Secure. Safe. But all of me churns for something else." Savannah suddenly had the courage to face her parents. "I want a different life, a wider world."

A tear rolled down Mother's cheek.

"I'm sorry, Mother."

Mother shook her head, not in disgust or anger, but— Savannah couldn't place it, puzzled over the linger in Mother's gaze.

Father moved to the chair Savannah had occupied, reached for Mother's hand.

Mother pulled out a handkerchief from her apron pocket.

"I know you don't understand. I know you must think me an ingrate . . . A while back—at my request—Lloyd took me to see alley dwellers and—"

"Took you where?" asked Father.

"Somewhere Southwest, a place called Beggars' Bay. As I said, I *asked* him to. See, he gave me this book—"

"Where else have you been with this Lloyd fellow?"

"Nowhere else, Father. Just to see alley dwellers and last night." Savannah swallowed. "My point is that . . . it's so awful the way those people live. There must be a change! And if last night taught me anything, it's that I *must* be part of that change! Part of making the world as it *ought* to be!"

"And how do you propose to do this?" asked Father.

"To be honest, I don't know." Savannah shifted from foot to foot, looked down at the floor. "I'm sorry if I'm a disappointment."

When she looked up she saw concern but not worry in Mother's, in Father's eyes.

"You are strong willed," said Father.

"You are daring," said Mother. "You are many things, but you are *not* a disappointment. You remind me so much of me when I was young."

Savannah was stunned.

Mother and Father looked at each other.

"It's time," Mother said to Father.

Father nodded. "Savannah, go up and check on the boy—what's his name again?"

"Bim."

"Go check on Bim, then join us back down here, please."

MOTHER QUESTING

Hours later Savannah sat slumped on her bed.

Elbows on knees.

Chin in hands.

Numb.

Mind a cyclone.

Mother wasn't raised in Charleston but in Savannah.

Mother was the daughter of a woman born in slavery and a woman who was a—

Mother teased, tormented into quitting school. Teaching herself with secondhand books. Petrified whenever in a house where her only place of peace was a small attic with a single small dormer window, a house of sin and lust, drinking, laudanum, cussing, white men trying to grope her.

Mother left home at *fourteen*.

Mother not born with the vaunted name of Victoria, but the humble Essie.

And the woman with the troubled arm—not Dinah. Binah, Mother's one and only friend.

And Ma Clara, Mother's first lifeline, rescue, a bandy-legged woman with twinkling eyes, gray hair like a crown, skin darker than a moonless winter midnight.

Ma Clara who got her that job at a Miss Abby's boarding-house. Then came the benefactor.

That wealthy aunt no aunt, no kin at all, but a woman who went about helping people, especially young women, rise in life.

Savannah tried to picture Mother about the same age she was now, leaving *everything, everybody* she knew behind, setting sail into an unknown world with a woman she barely knew.

Mother questing.

Savannah closed her eyes, strained to see young Mother during those lonely, lonely days, weeks, months, in a row house with first-floor blue shutters askew, in some Baltimore back street, enduring grueling lessons—etiquette, deportment, elocution, fancy food, table settings, how to dress—on everything she needed to enter the world of the likes of the Sandersons in Washington, DC. And sketching had been such a solace and salvation for Mother just as it was for her.

The face of another girl floated by: of that girl Savannah had seen in Beggars' Bay, that girl in a faded red-check pinafore dress with a proud, alert bearing, that girl sweeping three crude wooden steps.

What if she had a benefactor? Who might she become?

"So you see, my darling girl, I know very well what a hard life is," Mother had said at one point.

"Savannah, if you want to turn your back on the life we offer, we ask that you think long and hard," Father had added.

And their words had merged, blended together.

"Opportunity is nothing to sneeze at."

"You think those folks you saw in that alley wouldn't want what you have?"

"We can't lock you up in your room."

"We can't make you do anything really."

"Before you know it, Savannah, you will be a woman."

"We want you to be happy. But we want you to take care about the way you want to go. The kind of life you want to have."

"And the sacrifices you are willing to make to live that life."

"When you go out into the world, you must do so with eyes wide open."

"We ask one thing."

"Finish high school."

When Mother told Savannah that months back she had actually met her benefactor, she just stared unblinking, suddenly seeing herself in Uncle Madison's shop and the frail but erect sprite of a woman with that fiery, ancient gaze.

Seeing the woman clutch her pearl and diamond butterfly brooch, how her eyes went tender, misted up.

"Her name is Dorcas Vashon. We had a discreet lunch that week," said Mother. "She told me that she met you at Madison's."

What a lovely encounter this has been . . . A lovely encounter indeed.

"And you named me Savannah . . ."

"A piece of home. A way of keeping with me the good I did know there, a way of remembering the people who showed me love, knew me best, helped make me strong."

"I'll be right back," said Mother at the tail end of a long silence. When she returned, she had a small black velvet pouch. From it she brought out a necklace: a single strand of coral beads. "My mother gave me this when I was nine. A birthday gift, the only time I can remember her ever paying me close attention."

Mother pressed the necklace into Savannah's hands.

"According to Mamma, coral was a talisman against harm."

Savannah rolled the beads between her fingers.

"Mamma snatched it from my neck the day I left home to work at Miss Abby's. I can still hear their pitter-patter. I later found the beads after Mamma died, kept them. But then when I left Savannah with Dorcas Vashon, as I stood out on the ship's deck, I started to toss the beads into the sea."

"What stopped you?" asked Savannah.

"A feeling, something that didn't fully come to me until much later."

"And it was?"

"Maybe Mamma did the best she could. And maybe I got some of my grit from her."

It started to all make sense.

The pride in things like Tiffany candlesticks.

The overprotectiveness.

The anger at Charlie turning his back on the security of Father's firm.

"Charlie knows?" Savannah had asked at one point.

Mother nodded.

Before heading up to her room, Savannah telephoned Charlie, told him about Harrison, her harrowing night, Lloyd, the Hell Fighters, Bim. And—

"They just told me about Mother . . . Her past . . . How did you feel when they told you? . . ."

She lowered her voice even more.

"Wait—you actually called her a hypocrite? . . . Wow! . . . How do I feel? . . . I don't know how I feel . . . Angry? . . . No. Really I'm still in shock."

After she hung up the telephone, Savannah thought about Charlie calling Mother a hypocrite. She didn't agree.

The Sandersons, your parents, everybody else there last night—these people have worked darn hard for what they have.

Savannah had always regarded Mother as an ornament, bauble, the weaker one. Now she was reckoning with the fact that Mother was so much stronger, braver than she had ever imagined. Mother fought, forged on. She wasn't content with *pegging out an existence.* Mother had indeed *made a life!* She was as fierce, as noble as Nannie Burroughs.

"And, perhaps," Savannah whispered to herself, "if I ever have a daughter, perhaps I'll name her Essie."

Savannah rose from her bed, stepped over to her window to take in dusk descending.

Lost in thought over Mother's bitter, difficult childhood, Savannah didn't hear the telephone ring, didn't hear Father's fast footsteps up the stairs, only—

"Savannah!"

When she reached the landing, she saw Father heading for Charlie's old room.

She followed, frantic. "What is it now?!"

EENY, MEENY

There's likely to be more trouble tonight."

By then Father had a sleeping Bim in his arms. "Grab the Bayer."

Father had just settled Bim on the davenport in the living room when there was a knock on the back door.

"I'll get it," said Father.

Oscar Holloway.

"I've plenty of plywood to spare," Savannah heard him say. "Come take what you need."

While Father boarded up windows, Savannah helped Mother shuttle blankets, pillows, candles, food, dishes, utensils, down to the basement, where she grabbed Charlie's old baseball bat near Father's old-timey desk.

Later, by candlelight they supped on Campbell's chicken soup and Sunshine Krispy crackers.

By candlelight too they listened to the terror of sounds in the distance.

Eeny, meeny, miny, moe!
Catch a—

Sirens.
Gunshots.
Shouts.
Other sounds of malice, of mayhem.
Sky raining glass.
Savannah was in that crevice of an alley all over again.
This is not as the world ought to be! She gripped an invisible
lead pipe in her hand.

Eeny, meeny, miny, moe!
Catch a—

She nodded off, jerked awake, nodded off, caught glimpses
of Father pacing, Mother, Father holding hands, smelled
another candle lit, heard Bim mumble in his sleep on the pallet beside hers, woke with the dawn, then upstairs with Mother,
with Father, saw their street had been spared.

But evil roamed free elsewhere in the capital the next night
too.

If he hollers, cut his throat.

During those days of savage, curdling rage Savannah steadied herself mostly by tending to Bim. Feeding him chicken or oxtail soup, checking his brow for temperature, icing his ankle, fluffing the pillow beneath that ankle, reading to him from one of her old books. Fairy tales by Hans Christian Andersen. Frank Baum's *The Road to Oz*.

"Thank you, Miss Fine Lady," the boy always said.

"Bim, my name is Savannah. You call me that, okay?" she said at one turn.

"Okay, Miss Fine Lady."

During daylight calm, Father stashed canned food in the Buick, had Mother and Savannah pack overnight bags. But they didn't have to flee their home. With Tuesday came troops, then a pouring, purging rain.

And telephone call after telephone call.

It was early afternoon when Mother and Father withdrew to their bedroom, closed the door.

From the other side Savannah listened to Father relay grim news those telephone calls bore.

Negro men, women, children dragged from streetcars yards from the Capitol, the White House, skulls fractured with rifle butts, souls crawling to safety through bloodstained streets, whites shooting from terror cars, Negroes shooting from terror cars, stabbings, old woman beaten to a pulp, old man on his knees in the doorway of a D Street shop begging for mercy.

Savannah imagined her parents sitting on their bed, Father's head in his hands, Mother rubbing his shoulders.

"Dr. Woodson tucked, just in the nick of time, into the darkened doorway of a store near Pennsylvania Avenue," said Father with such a heavy heart. "But nearby another man was not so lucky. Woodson saw a gang of white soldiers snatch him up as one would a beef for slaughter, shot him point-blank."

Father spoke of damages to businesses, to homes, who needed to get bailed out of jail, who needed help for a burial, with medical bills, with tiding over until able to return to work. Of President Woodrow Wilson on his yacht with dysentery and once back in the White House, needing his rest.

Listening in, Savannah surprised herself. No tears. No trembling. Something within told her that if she could survive this madness—

She went back downstairs and stepped outside her house. No damage to any houses on her block. No broken glass, rocks, pools of blood on her part of M Street NW.

Later that day, after Calvin Chase, John Lewis, Hannibal Bash, Waylon Jones, and Mr. Holloway trooped into the living room, before Father closed the sliding doors, Savannah asked, "Will you have a lot of claims to pay out?"

"Not sure, but I don't expect it to be so bad. Most of the damage is in Southwest." Father hung his head. "A lot of folks there can't afford insurance."

The Walcotts?

The Fletchers?

Spencer?

All her brave Hell Fighters—how had they fared?

Savannah rushed to the telephone, told the operator that she didn't know the number.

"It's a grocery store, Southwest. Name's Fletcher."

LIKE A WILDFIRE LEAPS A RIVER

Like a wildfire leaps rivers, shift-shapes, turns into tornadoes of flames, so rage leaped from city to city.

"CHICAGO RIOTS EXTEND TO 'LOOP' DISTRICT," reported the *Star* on July 29. "DEATHS NOW TOTAL 24."

On and on and—

Savannah reached her limit, stopped reading newspapers altogether at one point. When she went back, she kept it to light reading. Ads. Poetry. One day it was a short story about a strong-willed, beguiling, and impish beauty, Roxana, who much to everyone's surprise married a plodder named Dick, a man she had wrapped around her little finger.

"Red summer had merged into a fall resplendent in a galaxy of yellow and browns, and Dick trudged home from the depot thru the cooler atmosphere, so pleasingly refreshing after the long, hot day just over. The day's work—"

Savannah paused, went back. *Red summer merged.*

The writer meant something wondrous by that, but for Savannah that phrase "Red Summer" brought only unbridled brutality to mind, had her on the brink of tears, churning over a way to strike back, wondering if she'd have to live in fear for the rest of her life, always braced for news of more evil unloosed.

Red Summer.

Tidying her room, sketching on her balcony, or going through her wardrobe for clothing—not that she was tired of, but that she simply didn't need—Savannah constantly asked, *Why? What have we ever done to them?*

Money. Power. It's always one or the other. Or both.

"And there's the fear," Savannah whispered.

Weeks later, a mended Bim was ready to be driven to the Walcotts'.

"So everyone's all right?" Savannah asked on the early August day when Lloyd came through those recessed double doors with crocheted curtains to their three-quarter-length panes, as he stepped down those stairs with latticed risers in something like a fleur-de-lis pattern.

When she'd gotten through to Mr. Fletcher after calm came to the capital, he had said Lloyd had been by and that his family was fine. But Mr. Fletcher didn't know about the others.

"They all come through fine," Lloyd now assured her on that early August day.

As Savannah stood there, Bim's hand in hers, she saw the Walcotts' street hadn't come through fine. There were some boarded-up windows and busted Millet post streetlamps.

"Mr. Walcott will see you home," said Savannah, glancing down at Bim.

Tears welled up in the boy's eyes; he grabbed Savannah around the waist. "Please, Miss Fine Lady, please let me stay with you."

"I can't do that, Bim. But I'll visit. I promise." She stroked his face, then released the boy's hand into Lloyd's. In the exchange their own hands touched. Savannah looked over her shoulder, saw Father with eyes facing front. She went on tiptoe, kissed Lloyd on the cheek, then pressed hers against his. "How, when will we—"

"We'll figure something out, Miss Ting."

As the black Buick pulled off, Savannah looked back, once again touched by the way Lloyd led Bim down the street.

And when Savannah returned home, she overheard something she likened to the rising of the sun.

MORE CAPITAL ARRESTS

I made a terrible mistake and I'm sorry . . . No, Charlie, I was overbearing and . . ."

Mother apologizing?

"You—you deserve to live your life under no cloud of condemnation . . . With this world on fire, we all must take happiness wherever we find it."

Mother forgiving?

Mother as she ought to be?

Turmoil. Tragedy. That's what it took to bring this about. There was guilt bundled up with Savannah's gratitude. Her family was becoming whole while so many lives were being torn apart in a world that *was* still so very much on fire.

Red Summer had merged into a Red Fall.

Ellenton, South Carolina . . . Omaha, Nebraska . . .

More working people were rising up!

Strike!

Police in Boston.

Steelworkers in Ohio.

Coal miners in Illinois.

And there was the stepped-up hunt for radicals. In Akron, Baltimore, Saint Louis—all around the nation it seemed. Then came the headline that sent a chill down Savannah's spine: "MORE CAPITAL ARRESTS THIS AFTER-NOON, SAY JUSTICE DEPT. AGENTS."

The next day Bim showed up at the Riddles' back door with a note from Nella.

Savannah knew, knew in her gut, that it wasn't about Miss Gertie falling ill again, wasn't about some Poro products. Tears were on the rise and her hands were trembling as she removed the note from its envelope.

HIS "MISS TING"

Father! Father!"

Savannah rushed to the backyard where Father was pulling up tomato stakes, readying what was left of the plants for rubbish.

"Father! Lloyd has been arrested!"

Father reached out to Calvin Chase for help but again and again—nothing but the runaround. Then came the telephone call that sent Savannah to her knees.

Deported?

Lloyd was from Saint Thomas. Savannah couldn't make any sense of it.

The United States had purchased the Danish West Indies a few years back, renamed them the Virgin Islands. People on Saint John, Saint Croix, Saint Thomas—they were *American citizens*.

Then she heard Lloyd.

Born in Barbados, but a while back I moved to Saint Thomas.

Later, listless, tearless, blind to townhouse turrets and gables, treetops, Millet post streetlamps, she stood on her balcony, mourning words unsaid, missing the sound of his "Miss Ting."

MURMURATION

It was the season when oaks, birches, lindens, maples shed red, orange, yellow leaves, create coverlets for ground atop their feet.

A time when twilight bids swarms of starlings, boat-tailed grackles, red-winged blackbirds to make magic in the sky.

Fluttering, twirling, swirling, twisting, rising, falling, reeling, swooping, whirling, flinging themselves into pirouettes, grand jetés, then, for a moment in time, flocking, in no way timorous, into a spectacular, fantastical shape—whale, seahorse, prehistoric beast.

From her balcony Savannah stood amazed at what it meant.

"It is called a murmuration," she heard nasally Mr. Neval tell her class years back.

During this season of murmurations, Savannah let her parents know when she planned to visit Nella and Miss Gertie. During one visit, she inquired about that bready thing, that cross between a doughnut and a biscuit that had tasted so good.

Bakes, she learned.

The name, along with how to make the batter and fry them up.

Whether morning, afternoon, or evening, Savannah walked to, from Southwest intrepid, took delight when she ran into Spencer, Glenna even. Sometimes Savannah popped in on the Fletchers and left with wax paper packets of pickled pigs' feet.

Constantly she thought about how Mother had started with nothing.

Would you rather you lived in a shack with an outhouse out back?

No, I would not! Savannah thought one day en route to old man Boudinot's, a place she frequented often, scanning the shelves for books about Africa, the West Indies, India, ordering titles the squirrelly old man thought she might like, plucking from a shelf, now and then, a book that quietly beckoned. *The Heart of a Woman*, a slim volume of verse, was one.

"The author, Georgia Douglas Johnson, she's local, you know," said old man Boudinot as Savannah handed him four Walking Liberties. "Lives over on South Street," he added.

From musing on Mother's "nothing," Savannah thought even harder on how she might take the SO much that was in her lap, within her grasp, and fashion it into a force for the way things *ought* to be.

She read up on socialism, communism, wondering if she

could really fully embrace either. After all, while her mind often wandered in church, deep down she did believe in God.

Savannah didn't much study anarchism. For one, she wanted nothing to do with bombs.

Practical knowledge—she sought that too.

"No, Charlie, I mean if you didn't have the studio, how much would your rent be?"

She tallied up what her allowance came to a year.

"Well, about how much do you spend on groceries a week? . . . Do things costs the same in New York as they do here?"

She sounded out her parents about how much they spent on clothing for her a year. Later, looking through her wardrobe, chiffonier, dresser, she knew she really wouldn't *need* any new clothing for two, maybe three years.

More questions for Charlie: "Where is Hubert Harrison's Liberty League headquartered? . . . How far is that from you? . . . The magazine the *Crusader*? How far is that from you? . . . Do you know the editor?"

She visited Uncle Madison—"Charlie has told me about a school called Cooper Union where I can study art for free."

And Savannah had not abandoned Lincoln Heights. On more than one autumn day she took the streetcar there to help her friends break down garden plots, corral leaves, save seeds for next year.

And she had questions for them too.

The cost, the length of a voyage to Haiti, to Liberia?

Would Principal Burroughs ever let someone with just a high school diploma teach at her school?

Probably not, Savannah said to herself a beat before Mona shrugged.

And maybe, Savannah reckoned, maybe going to Howard wasn't such a bad idea after all. She began to see herself, not as an art major—

Methinks I see . . .

"Mother," she asked one day. "What course of study must one take to be a journalist?"

And photography . . . maybe she'd take it up after all, apprentice with Uncle Madison, not with an eye on mastering the portraiture of prominent race men and women, not to cover events like the Sandersons' fete, but to document lives that newspapers ignored. The forgettable, the forgotten.

During these days of thinking, asking, reading, questing, seeking, Savannah was most proud of getting Yolande out to Lincoln Heights.

Raking leaves, stuffing them into croker sacks, breathing in all that crisp autumn air, attending a Friday night social, a lecture by Dr. Woodson—Yolande was truly renewed.

Saturdays when not out at Lincoln Heights, Savannah made a point of spending some time with Yolande.

A photoplay.

A meal at Gaskins'.

Sometimes both.

To, from Dunbar they walked, often arm in arm.

During one of those walks, Savannah hit upon something else to do, something that might not be wholly impossible.

Methinks I see . . . mewing her mighty youth.

First she spoke with Nella.

ON THE EDISON AMBEROLA

Mother, Father, Savannah were in the living room, dinner done, dusk on duty.

Playing on the Edison Amberola was the brassy, bluesy "Indianola" by Lieutenant Jim Europe and his Hell Fighters Band.

Savannah cleared her throat, spoke her hope.

Father, his thinking face on, said nothing for the longest while.

"What brought this on?" Mother finally asked. She looked shocked, but not repulsed—nothing like when Savannah broached the subject of helping out at Nannie Burroughs's school.

"What brought this on?" responded Savannah. "The difference your Ma Clara and Dorcas Vashon made in your life. The notion that there are things that need to cease immediately and then there are our far-off hopes and dreams."

"The grandfather would, of course, have to agree," said Mother.

"We would need Calvin or another attorney to draw up papers so that all is decent and in order," added Father.

"I will take him to and from school. I will help him with his homework. You can take most or all of what you'd spend on clothing for me and . . ."

"Let us sleep on it," said Mother.

"That's all I ask," replied Savannah.

In a few days' time, Mother and Father said yes to adopting Bim.

MOST OF ALL THERE IS LOVE

There is roast goose, braised ham, lamb chops.

There's parsley new potatoes, peas, carrots. Brussels sprouts too.

A pumpkin pie, a strawberry shortcake, along with miniature custards grace the burl and marquetry buffet opposite the dining room table around which there had been prayer.

For family. For life and limb.

For strength of mind.

Friendship.

As platters and serving bowls are passed around this table laid with Tiffany candlesticks and two sets of salt and pepper cellars, there is laughter too.

Most of all there is love.

That of two handsome middle-aged couples and a man in his thirties with a Charlie Chaplin mustache and probing eyes—an ebullient fellow who insisted on taking photographs of the spread before everyone took their seats.

There is the love of a bright-smiling lad in a tweed Dubbelbilt suit and with more meat on his bones than he had a few months back. And of a young woman in a royal-blue taffeta dress chattering away about the last meeting of the Bethel Junior Literary Society. By her side sits another young woman. This one wears an emerald-green velvet dress with an overlay of emerald-green chiffon. Around her neck, a string of coral beads.

Next to her, tickling her from time to time, sits another man in his thirties. Tall, angular, dark, velvety skin, razor-thin mustache. His hair is pomaded. He has on a nice suit.

Yes, Charlie came home for Christmas.

On Monday, December 29, 1919, two days before her eighteenth birthday, Savannah Riddle sat in the Madeline Beauty Parlor very much in an *Excelsior!* state of mind.

What part in this great drama of the future . . . ?

And Savannah was crystal clear about the part that she would play—and how she would *make a life.*

She removed *The Heart of a Woman* from her handbag, flipped to page fifty-six, and for the umpteenth time read "Pendulum."

About swinging to "the uttermost reaches of pain."

About "the echo of sighs," a "deluge of rain."

About rebounding "to the limits of bliss."

And also about "an infinite kiss."

From the pages of the book she brought out an envelope with a winsome stamp: against a background of coral red, a two-horse chariot speeds a sovereign across a sea.

Just as with "Pendulum," Savannah read the letter for the umpteenth time.

Dear Miss Ting,
  I hope this finds you still brave. As for me, I've had the good fortune to find work at . . .

When the Madeline Beauty Parlor's proprietor, Madame Mary M. Smith, had Savannah's hair in her hands—hair shampooed, conditioned by staff—the regal caramel-colored woman sighed. "Are you *sure* you want to do this, Savannah? There are girls who would kill to have your hair."

"She's sure," said Mother, glancing up from a recent *Crisis.*

"If you say so, Mrs. Riddle."

Madame Mary M. Smith then picked up a pair of scissors, proceeded to clip, clip, clip, snip, snip, snip her way to giving Savannah a Dutch bob.

Savannah looked into the mirror, studied the woman's handiwork, watched hair fall, float to the checkerboard floor.

AUTHOR'S NOTE

The year 1919 was a long goodbye to the Great War, as World War I was called, with its 37 million civilian and military casualties. That year also saw the waning of an influenza pandemic in which possibly as many as 50 million people died worldwide (and which, by the way, didn't originate in Spain, but in Kansas). And there was so much more in that single year.

Revolutionaries reacted to the status quo with bombs.

Suffragists rallied around and roared for passage of the Anthony amendment so that women in America would have the national vote.

And New Negro sentiment surged.

And conservatives railed against certain immigrants.

And progressive workers sought to unite in the fight for better working conditions and better pay too.

And in the spring, summer, and fall of 1919, there was that horrific spate of race riots, more than twenty in all.

In his book *1919*, William K. Klingaman called it "the year our world began."

A "year that changed America"—that's what Martin W. Sandler dubbed it in his book also titled *1919*.

February 17, 1919: The 369th infantry regiment marches up Fifth Avenue in New York City. Today the regiment is often called the Harlem Hellfighters, but back circa 1919 they were more commonly called simply the Hell Fighters.

As a child of the turbulent 1960s, with its civil rights, black power, women's liberation, and antiwar movements—and with its riots—I wondered, *What was it like to be a young woman in 1919? To witness such a hurricane of events without realizing that you* are *in fact part of history?*

Savannah came to me as a privileged young woman in a nose dive of discontent. Discontent with her life, her social set, with what others think she *ought* to be, do, want. She's pulsing for change, new vistas, while facing some frightening events.

As I imagined Savannah's life, troops of historical figures came parading through in person and by mention: Booker T. Washington; Frederick Douglass; scholar-activist W. E. B.

Du Bois; Carter G. Woodson, the "father" of black history; millionaire Madam C. J. Walker, whose company provided thousands of black people with jobs. As did the St. Louis–based Poro, another black-owned beauty-care company, the one for which Nella Walcott is a sales rep. At its helm was the tenacious Annie Turnbo Malone, for whom Madam C. J. Walker (née Sarah Breedlove) once worked.

Into *Saving Savannah* also strode firebrand Nannie Helen Burroughs. She opened her Lincoln Heights school for young women in 1909, the same year that Du Bois, Ida Wells-Barnett, Mary Church Terrell, and several white activists founded the NAACP.

Circa 1900–1920: Nannie Helen Burroughs, born in Orange, Virginia. In 1964, her school was renamed the Nannie Helen Burroughs School.

Burroughs, fierce feminist—someone who did "specialize in the wholly impossible"—is not as well known as she ought to be. Often when the subject is the early-twentieth-century suffragist movement, typically *if* black women are mentioned . . .

Maybe journalist and antilynching crusader Ida Wells-Barnett, who launched the first black woman's suffrage organization (Chicago's Alpha Suffrage Club in 1913).

Maybe the millionaire's daughter Mary Church Terrell, a founder and first president of the organization to which Mrs. Riddle belongs, the National Association of Colored

Women formed in 1896 (today's National Association of Colored Women's Clubs). Outside of academia, rarely is Nannie Helen Burroughs mentioned.

Burroughs is just one of legions of today's lesser-known early-twentieth-century DC lights, agents of change on so many fronts at a time when Jim Crow was so virulent.

Before the Great War: Students at Nannie Burroughs's
National Training School for Women and Girls.

Portraits of black life under Jim Crow rightly present the abuse and humiliations endured, the possibilities denied, the potential stymied, but many portraits stop there, leaving the impression that all black people—or most—were downtrodden, living lives of quiet desperation and deprivation. When black agency is brought into view, the focus is usually on lawsuits, marches, and boycotts.

But there's more to the story. More than the efforts of the Du Boises and others who are household names today.

When you dig deeper into history, you find troops of black people—people galled by Jim Crow, people who loathed Jim Crow—people whose names rarely show up in the history books. People like Savannah's parents. People to so admire for the things they did when *don't* prevailed. In doing well for themselves, they delivered a whole lot of good to their people.

This unsung black phalanx did more than dream a world. It created one. In 1919, black DC (soon to be supplanted by Harlem as the "capital of black America," as the "Mecca") had much to offer her people, especially in its famous U Street corridor, with Howard University the crown jewel.

So maybe white newspapers weren't always kind to black people or gave them short shrift. Savannah and her family had, among other newspapers, the *Washington Bee* with the slogan "Sting for Our Enemies—Honey for Our Friends." Launched in 1882, this weekly endured for forty years, until 1922, a year after the death of its editor, lawyer William Calvin Chase.

When black people of means from New York City or Chicago or from San Francisco visited DC, no they couldn't stay at a first-rate white-owned hotel, but then John White-law Lewis, laborer turned excellent entrepreneur, stepped in. Shortly before the Riddles' 1919 Christmas dinner, Lewis's five-story, U-shaped brick-and-limestone hotel and apartment building (twenty-two hotel rooms and twenty-five rental units) opened at 13th and T Streets. This Italian Renaissance Revival style structure was designed by black architect Isaiah T. Hatton, a graduate of M Street School. During the week of the Whitelaw's grand opening, the *Bee* reported that some seven thousand people turned out—dressed to the nines—for a series of public programs.

And if guests at the Whitelaw wanted a fine dining experience outside of the hotel, thanks to other enterprising black minds, they had options, as did Savannah, her family, her friends. One was Gaskins' Cafe and Lunch at 320 8th Street NW, "the House of Quality and Service." Another was Dade's Palace Cafe at 1216 Pennsylvania Avenue NW.

While A. J. Gaskins and Moses H. Dade created places where black people could dine in dignity, others catered to different needs. Mr. Pinchback's men's clothing store was inspired by ads I came across in the *Bee* for Robert Harlan's Toggery Shop at 1848 Seventh near the corner of T Street. While my description of beautician Mary M. Smith is fictional, her establishment, the Madeline Beauty Parlor, was real, located at 905 U Street.

Circa 1912 and circa 1907: Annie Brooks Evans (left) and her daughter Lillian Evans, both by Addison N. Scurlock.

While black do-ers in DC were building businesses and institutions they were readying their young to pursue success in a range of fields.

Take soprano Lillian Evans, one of whose concerts Yolande and her parents attend. Shortly after *Saving Savannah* ends, Evans became an internationally renowned concert singer. Stage name: Lillian Evanti. Her mother, Annie Brooks Evans, a photograph of whom Savannah sees on display in Madison Spurlock's window, was a music teacher in DC public schools. Lillian's father, physician William Bruce Evans, was the founding principal of Armstrong Manual Training School, one of DC's two high schools for black students when Savannah was a teen. Armstrong (which in 1925 became Armstrong Technical High School, and today is called Friendship Armstrong Academy) was where one of DC's most famous sons, Duke Ellington, studied art and design.

1917: Dunbar High from the March 1917 *Crisis*.

(The career of this legendary composer and bandleader will take off after his move to the Big Apple in 1923.)

Hallie E. Queen, who held a bachelor's degree from Cornell University and a master's from Stanford University, and who did speak several languages, was likely not one of black DC's favorite daughters.

Queen began working for the Department of Military Intelligence when America entered the Great War. Documents attesting to her spying on the black community include a September 1917 memo on her findings while in New York City. Example: a German doctor trying to recruit black physicians for the German medical corps. Queen also warned that William Monroe Trotter of Boston, civil rights activist and publisher of the *Guardian*, "was a radical colored man who might make trouble." This was, as historian Mark Ellis has pointed out, "undeniably true but also common knowledge." Hallie E. Queen was apparently not much of a sleuth and prone to wild imaginings. (And, by the way, Miss Queen was at Madam C. J. Walker's 1918 Christmas party, which Savannah's brother, Charlie, covered.)

From high-profile to everyday people, one of the greatest chroniclers of black DC during Savannah's days (and beyond) was Addison N. Scurlock, the man on whom I based Savannah's play uncle, Madison Spurlock.

1908: Halle E. Queen from a Cornell University yearbook.

Addison N. Scurlock, a native of Fayetteville, North Carolina, was in his

Circa 1910–1920: Addison N. Scurlock.

late teens when, around 1900, his family moved to DC. There, he apprenticed with a white photographer. Then, in 1911, Addison opened his first studio at 900 U Street. Sons Robert and George followed in his footsteps and, thankfully, the Scurlock legacy has been preserved, cared for by the National Museum of American History. This treasure trove includes roughly 200,000 prints, negatives, and color transparencies. That's a whole lot of history, a whole lot of insight on the rest of the story, a source of gems to be found when we dig deeper into history.

For *Saving Savannah*, I also had to dig into the New Negro Movement, a militant call for social justice combined with reaches into black folkways and back to Africa for artistic inspiration—a movement that began before 1919 and one that was hardly confined to Harlem. Although drawing on deep roots, this movement, with its future-looking gaze, was more of a birth than a rebirth or renaissance. Here I thought about a tendency to see the movement as African American–made and to overlook the contributions of people from the black diaspora, especially West Indians. That is, other than perhaps the Jamaican poet Claude McKay and Marcus Garvey, also Jamaican and founder of the Universal Negro Improvement Association.

Digging deeper, I stumbled upon the firebrand born on the tiny Leeward Island Nevis, Cyril Briggs. And thanks to the NYPL Digital Collection, I was able to view copies of Briggs's magazine, the *Crusader*, with those covers featuring young women that so entranced Savannah.

And then I became fascinated with Hubert Henry Harrison of St. Croix—such a beacon light for Savannah, a man whose life was cut short in 1927 due to complications around an appendectomy. At the outset I knew Harrison's name but not what an amazing mind he had, not that he was called the "black Socrates," not why independent scholar Jeffrey B. Perry hails him as "The Voice of Harlem Radicalism."

Circa 1919: Hubert Henry Harrison.

This is just some of what went into—what I got caught up with—when building Savannah's world and her entrance into the Jazz Age.

Flappers.

Rising hemlines.

Drop-waist dresses.

The shedding of corsets.

Frenzied dancing until dawn.

Sheet music from 1919: Arranger, composer, and bandleader James Reese Europe, who attended DC's M Street School (forerunner of Dunbar High), was a major figure on the ragtime/jazz scene. Before the Great War, Europe's Clef Club Orchestra was the first to play jazz at New York City's Carnegie Hall (1912). His Society Orchestra is believed to be the first black band to cut a record (1913). His band often accompanied the famous white dancing duo Irene and Vernon Castle of fox-trot fame. The legendary songwriter team Noble Sissle and Eubie Blake were among the members of Europe's bands.

More women behind the wheels of cars.

And in this new era, with women (and some men) celebrating the ratification then adoption to the Constitution of the Anthony amendment turned the Nineteenth Amendment (August 18, 1920), and with the NAACP, the NACW, and other organizations soldiering on in the civil rights crusade, I do wonder how Savannah Riddle will make her mark.

For sure, I can see her making her way to Georgia Douglas Johnson's townhouse at 1461 South Street NW to get her copy of *The Heart of a Woman* autographed. And who knows, perhaps Savannah will become a denizen of the Saturday literary salon this poet and pioneering playwright hosted in her home.

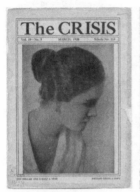  

Crisis Cover March 1920: According to Yale University, the photograph is of Georgia Douglas Johnson. Inside that March issue of the *Crisis* are two of her poems: "Attar" and "Afterglow." There's also this news: A new song, "I Want to Die While You Love Me," is issued by the Ricordi music house of New York. The lyric is by Georgia Douglas Johnson and the music is by H. T. Burleigh.

Crisis Cover November 1919: This is the issue Mother is perusing while sitting in the beauty parlor waiting for her daughter to get that Dutch bob.

Crisis Cover February 1919: This is the issue Savannah flips through one Saturday night.

NOTES

For full citations of sources heavily consulted please see Selected Sources.

Page 7 "Camel trappings jingle . . .": "Hindustan," music by Harold Weeks, lyrics by Oliver Wallace, first recorded in 1918, https://www .sheetmusicbackinprint.com/popular/hindustan.html. Last accessed January 28, 2019.

Page 13 "U.S. AT WAR WITH GERMANY . . .": *Evening Star*, April 6, 1917, p.1.

Page 13 "Children the Pitiful Victims of Modern War's Ruthlessness": *Evening Star*, June 19, 1917, p. 1.

Page 13 "INSANITY INCREASE ATTRIBUTED TO WAR": *Washington Bee*, May 12, 1917, p. 2.

Page 13 "13 MILLION MEN IS COST OF WAR": *Washington Bee*, January 26, 1918, p. 3.

Page 14 4-Minute Men were volunteer propagandists for the Committee on Public Information created by President Woodrow Wilson to gin up support for the war.

Page 14 "SCANDINAVIA IS SWEPT BY 'SPANISH INFLUENZA' ": *Evening Star*, September 19, 1918, p. 9.

Page 14 "SPANISH INFLUENZA SPREADING IN D.C.": *Evening Star*, September 26, 1918, p. 2.

Page 15 On the frankfurter: For example, in an article on an upcoming 1918 Christmas program in Kensington, the *Philadelphia Inquirer* noted that "Liberty sausages before the days of the Hun were known as 'Frankfurters,' more familiarly to children as 'hot doggies.'" (December 21, 1918, p. 16.)

Page 15 On the hamburger: For one, by unanimous vote the Seattle Meat Dealers' Association abolished the term "hamburger" in favor of liberty steak in May 1918. "Order 'Liberty Steak' If You Want Hamburger," *Jackson Citizen Patriot*, May 4, 1918, p.1.

Page 15 "As a matter of fact . . .": "Puts O.K. on Sauerkraut," *Washington Bee*, July 27, 1918, p. 7.

Page 15 Items in comfort kit: *The Valve World*, June 1918, p. 188.

Page 15 Bombings in Philadelphia: They occurred on December 30, 1918. "Bombs Exploded in Judges' Homes," *Evening Star*, December 31, 1918, p. 4.

Page 16 New Year's Day suffragist protest: "President's Speeches Burned by Women in Rain," *Evening Star*, January 2, 1919, p. 18.

Page 16 On Ida Wells-Barnett in suffragist parade: This Woman Suffrage Procession was held on March 3, 1913. Ida Wells-Barnett was not the only black woman to march. Mary Church Terrell and twenty-two founders of the Delta Sigma Theta Sorority also marched.

Page 23 "MR. PRESIDENT, HOW LONG MUST WOMEN WAIT FOR LIBERTY?" and "MR. PRESIDENT, WHAT WILL YOU DO FOR WOMAN SUFFRAGE?": "Picketing for Suffrage," Library of Congress, https://www.loc.gov/item/today-in-history/august-28/. Last accessed January 28, 2019.

Page 24 "MAKE AMERICA SAFE FOR DEMOCRACY" and "RACE PREJUDICE IS THE OFFSPRING OF IGNORANCE AND THE MOTHER OF LYNCHING": "The Negro Silent Parade," *Crisis*, September 1917, pp. 241, 244.

Page 24 The Silent Parade: It was held on Saturday, July 28, 1917. An estimated eight to ten thousand black people participated in this protest. It began at Fifth Avenue and 59th Street and ended at 23rd Street and Madison Square. W. E. B. Du Bois was the architect of this parade.

Pages 44–47 Soldier on cover of *Crisis*, ads for colleges, Men of the Month column, "LYNCHING RECORD FOR THE YEAR 1918," "Private Harry Thomas . . .": *Crisis*, February 1919, cover, pp. 160, 161, 177–178, 180–181, 193, 202, 204, 205, http://www.modjourn.org/render.php?id=1292952614561750&view=mjp_object. Last accessed January 28, 2019.

Page 47 Charlie's letter about the Hell Fighters: Almost verbatim "All New York Joins to Pay Honor to 'Hell Fighters' in Parade on Fifth Avenue," *Evening World*, February 17, 1919, p. 1.

Pages 50, 51 ads for records, books, Lula Robinson, Idlewild, and busts: *Crisis*, February 1919, pp. 202, 204, 205, http://www.modjourn.org/render.php?id=1292952614561750&view=mjp_object.

Page 71 "All Warsaw in darkness. . . . gun fight!": *Washington Herald*, March 1, 1919, p. 1.

Page 72 Bombing in Southside Chicago: "Negro Dies, Many Hurt, in Bomb Explosion," *Washington Times*, February 28, 1919, p. 16.

Page 72 Bombing in Massachusetts: "I.W.W. Dynamiters Die in Explosion," *New York Times*, March 2, 1919, p. 9.

Page 76 Flyer for Burroughs's school: Almost verbatim from an ad in the *Washington Bee*, August 15, 1914, p. 6.

Page 76 Covers of the *Crusader*: https://digitalcollections.nypl.org/items/510d47df-a135-a3d9-e040-e00a18064a99, https://digitalcollections.nypl.org/items/510d47df-a13a-a3d9-e040-e00a18064a99, https://digitalcollections.nypl.org/items/510d47df-a159-a3d9-e040-e00a18064a99. Last accessed January 28, 2019.

Page 81 "Greatest Negro High School in the World": J. C. Wright, "The New Dunbar High School," Washington, DC, March 1917, p. 221.

Page 110 Nannie Burroughs's speech: Some of it is almost verbatim from

Burroughs's article "Black Women and Reform" in the *Crisis*, August 1915, p. 187.

Page 112 "'by which all others are secured.'": Waldo E. Martin, *The Mind of Frederick Douglass*, p. 147.

Page 117 Du Bois's "Close Ranks": *Crisis*, July 1918, p. 111.

Page 127 "First, as workers, black and white. . . . Any race or class": A. Philip Randolph, "Our Reason for Being," *Messenger*, August 1919, History Matters: The US Survey Course on the Web, http://historymatters.gmu.edu/d /5125/. Last accessed January 8, 2019. This editorial appeared a few months after it appears in this novel, but I can imagine Randolph uttering such sentiments in spring 1919.

Page 130 "The world, as it ought to be": Hubert H. Harrison's "The New Politics for the New Negro," (September 1917), collected in *When Africa Awakes* (New York: The Porro Press, 1920), p. 40.

Pages 131, 132 "In the home of an Italian rag-picker. . . . Bottle Alley": Jacob A. Riis, from *How the Other Half Lives* (New York: Charles Scribner's Sons, 1890), pp. 51, 69, 1, 34, 63, 66.

Page 140 "U.S. HUNTS ANARCHISTS": *Evening Star*, May 1, 1919, p. 1.

Page 141 "THE LARGEST BLOUSE DEPARTMENT IN THE CITY": *Evening Star*, May 1, 1919, p. 2.

Page 156 Lynchings outside Pickens, Mississippi: "Mob Lynches Negro Couple," *Washington Times*, May 9, 1919, p. 10.

Page 156 Man lynched near Dublin, Georgia: farmhand Jim Waters, on May 15, 1919, "Negro Assaulter of White Girl is Lynched by Mob," *Augusta Chronicle*, May 16, 1919, p. 1.

Page 156 Man burned alive near El Dorado, Arkansas: twenty-five-year-old Frank Livingston, a former soldier, on May 21, after he was forced to confess to the murder of his employer and his wife. "Frank Livingston (Lynching of)," Encyclopedia of Arkansas, http://www.encyclopediaofarkansas.net/encyclo pedia/entry-detail.aspx?entryID=8283. Last accessed January 9, 2019.

Page 156 Arson near Eatonton, Georgia: May 28, 1919, "Negro Buildings Near Eatonton Burned by Mob," *Augusta Chronicle*, May 29, 1919, p. 1.

Page 156 On the eclipse: "Eclipse of Sun Invisible in D.C.," *Washington Herald*, May 29, 1919, p. 5.

Page 161 "Blown to butcher's meat": Eyewitness to the aftermath of the bomb quoted in Cameron McWhirter, *Red Summer*, p. 55. The bomber's name was Carlo Valdinoci.

Page 162 On other bombings June 2–3, 1919: "Judges and Other Officials Marked for Bomb Attack," *Evening Star*, June 3, 1919, pp. 1–2.

Page 164 "BOMB AT ATTORNEY GENERAL'S HOME STARTS A NATION-WIDE ROUND-UP OF ANARCHISTS": *Evening Star* June 3, 1919, p. 1.

Page 164 "Fair, continued warm tonight": *Evening Star*, June 3, 1919, p. 1.

Page 165 "WOMAN SUFFRAGE WINS IN SENATE": *Evening Star*, June 5, 1919, p. 3.

Page 167 "THREE RADICALS TAKEN IN RAID BY DISTRICT POLICE": *Washington Herald*, June 15, 1919, p. 1.

Page 174 account of slave pen: E. S. Abdy, *Journal of a Residence and Tour in the United States of North America, from April, 1833, to October, 1834*, vol. 2 (London: J. Murray, 1835), pp. 96–97.

Page 178 On Harrison's intellect: Orator, journalist, educator, and NAACP field secretary William Pickens once described Harrison as "a plain black man who can speak more easily, effectively, and interestingly on a greater variety of subjects than any other man I have ever met in the great universities." Harrison was, said Pickens, a "'walking cyclopedia' of current facts" and it made "no difference" whether he was speaking about *Alice in Wonderland* or . . . the heaviest depths of Kant; about music, or art, or science, or political history." Jeffrey B. Perry, *Hubert Harrison: The Voice of Harlem Radicalism, 1883-1918*, p. 1.

Page 179 Harrison's address: Almost verbatim from "Our Larger Duty,"

When Africa Awakes, pp. 100–104. (The essay originally appeared in the August 1919 issue of *The New Negro*.)

Page 181 US Coins: Standing Liberty quarter minted 1916–1930; Walking Liberty quarter, 1916–1947; Winged Liberty dime also known as the Mercury dime, 1916–1945; and the Buffalo or Indian Head nickel 1913–1938.

Page 196 "POLICEMAN BATTLES WITH CRAZED NEGRO": *Washington Herald*, June 9, 1919, p. 1.

Page 196 "POSSES SEEK NEGRO WHO ATTACKED GIRL": *Washington Times*, July 6, 1919, p. 2.

Page 196 "NEGRO ROUND-UP WILL CONTINUE": *Washington Herald*, July 11, 1919, p. 1.

Page 208 Ace bandage: Oscar O. R. Schwidetzky, who at one point was director of a company that manufactured medical instruments and supplies, is credited with the invention of the All Cotton Elastic bandage in 1918.

Page 222 "as one would a beef for slaughter": These are Carter G. Woodson's words, from his affidavit on the DC riots, quoted in Cameron McWhirter, *Red Summer*, p. 100.

Page 224 "CHICAGO RIOTS. . . . DEATHS NOW TOTAL 24": *Evening Star,* July 29, 1919, p. 2.

Page 224 "Red summer had merged": Lincoln Rothblum, "The Reform of Roxana," *Topeka State Journal*, July 26, 1919, p. 12. Poetic license was taken here. I did not find this story in any DC papers. The spring-fall 1919 race riots in some two dozen cities were called "The Red Summer" by James Weldon Johnson in his book *Along This Way* (1933). Johnson, the "father" of the Black National Anthem, "Lift Every Voice and Sing," was field secretary for the NAACP when Savannah was a teen.

Page 228 "MORE CAPITAL ARRESTS": *Washington Times*, November 8, 1919, p. 1.

Page 239 "Pendulum": Georgia Douglas Johnson, *The Heart of a Woman and Other Poems* (Boston: Cornhill Company, 1918), p. 56.

Page 245 On the Whitelaw's opening week: "The Whitelaw Hotel," *Washington Bee*, November 29, 1919, pp. 1, 4.

Page 246 "the House of Quality and Service": ad, *Washington Bee*, January 4, 1919, p. 7.

Page 248 "was a radical colored man . . .": Herbert Parsons, Memorandum, September 29, 1917, p. 2, in Correspondence of the Military Intelligence Division Relating to "Negro Subversion," 1917–1941.

Page 248 "undeniably true but also common knowledge": Mark Ellis, *Race, War, and Surveillance: African Americans and the United States During World War I* (Bloomington: Indiana University Press, 2001), p. 57.

PHOTOGRAPH CREDITS

Page 242: Hell Fighters parade, Getty; **page 243:** Nannie Helen Burroughs, Library of Congress; **page 244:** Students at Nannie Burroughs's school, Getty; **page 246:** Annie Brooks Evans and Lillian Evans, Anacostia Community Museum, Smithsonian Institution; **page 247:** Dunbar High, the Modernist Journals Project (searchable database), Brown and Tulsa Universities, ongoing; **page 248:** Halle E. Queen, Cornell University Library; **page 249:** Addison N. Scurlock, Scurlock Studio Records, Archives Center, National Museum of American History, Smithsonian Institution; **page 250:** Hubert Henry Harrison, Photographs and Prints Division, Schomburg Center for Research in Black Culture, the New York Public Library; **page 251:** Sheet music, Library of Congress; **page 252:** Covers of the *Crisis*, the Modernist Journals Project (searchable database). Brown and Tulsa Universities, ongoing. http://www.modjourn.org.

SELECTED SOURCES

Bundles, A'Lelia. *On Her Own Ground: The Life and Times of Madam C. J. Walker*. New York: Washington Square Press, 2002.

Dagbovie, Pero Gaglo, PhD. *Carter G. Woodson in Washington, D.C.: The Father of Black History*. Charleston, SC: The History Press, 2014.

Easter, Opal V. *Nannie Helen Burroughs*. New York: Garland Publishing, 1995.

Hagedorn, Ann. *Savage Peace: Hope and Fear in America, 1919*. New York: Simon & Schuster, 2008.

Harrison, Hubert H. *When Africa Awakes: The "Inside Story" of the Stirrings and Strivings of the New Negro in the Western World*. New York: The Porro Press, 1920.

Jackson, Shantina Shannell. *"To Struggle and Battle and Overcome": The Educational Thought of Nannie Helen Burroughs, 1875–1961*, dissertation, University of California, Berkeley, Summer 2015.

Klingaman, William K. *1919: The Year Our World Began*. New York: HarperCollins, 1989.

McWhirter, Cameron. *Red Summer: The Summer of 1919 and the Awakening of Black America*. New York: Henry Holt, 2011.

Moore, Jacqueline M. *Leading the Race: The Transformation of the Black Elite in the Nation's Capital, 1880–1920*. Charlottesville: University of Virginia Press, 1999.

Perry, Jeffrey B. *Hubert Harrison: The Voice of Harlem Radicalism, 1883–1918*. New York: Columbia University Press, 2010.

Sandler, Martin W. *1919: The Year That Changed America*. New York: Bloomsbury, 2019.

Stewart, Alison. *First Class: The Legacy of Dunbar, America's First Black Public High School*. Chicago: Lawrence Hill Books, 2013.

Stewart, R.R.S. *Designing a Campus for African-American Females: The National Training School for Women and Girls 1907–1964*, thesis, University of Virginia, May 2008.

Taylor, Traki. L. "Woman Glorified: Nannie Helen Burroughs and the National Training School for Women and Girls, Inc., 1909–1961, *Journal of African American History*, vol. 87, (Autumn 2002), pp. 390–402.

ACKNOWLEDGMENTS

To my editor, Mary Kate Castellani, you were, as always, a dream to work with—always exuberant, always challenging, always thinking, always inspiring me, always keeping me from going down rabbit holes, getting too much sucked into history. Associate editor Claire Stetzer, thank you once again for your efficiency and for your grace. I'm also grateful to others in editorial: Cindy Loh and Annette Pollert-Morgan.

And once again what joy it was to work with the marvelous production editor Diane Aronson and the equally marvelous and intense copyeditor Patricia McHugh. I'm also grateful to production pros Melissa Kavonic and Nicholas Church as well as proofreader Regina Castillo.

In design: Donna Mark and Jeanette Levy. And then there's cover artist Connie Gabbert. Thank you!

And in marketing: Valentina Rice, Erica Barmash, Phoebe Dyer, Lily Yengle, and Alona Fryman.

And in sales: Frank Bumbalo, Brittany Bowler, and Daniel O'Connor.

And in publicity: Courtney Griffin and Erica Loberg.

And in school and library marketing: Beth Eller, Brittany Mitchell, and Jasmine Miranda.

It really does take a village! And Village Bloomsbury is, plain and simple, wondrous.

Thanks is also due to my sister, Nelta Gallemore, for carefully reading more than one draft, letting me pick your brain on fashion, and so much else; to friend and fellow writer Sharon G. Flake for being a terrific sounding board; to Barbados-born friend Karen Best for reviewing the manuscript for all things Bajan and especially for correcting my Bajan dialogue; to Haiti-born friend Dr. Mona Rigaud for assists with medical matters and Creole; to friend and fellow history lover John G. Sharp, retired Navy (military and civilian) for taking my questions on Washington, DC. And thank you Marian Mills at the American Philatelic Research Library for guiding me to the correct stamp!

Agent Jennifer Lyons, ever grateful for the way you champion my work.